The Hajji
and other stories

By the same author

The Visitation
The Emperor
Noorjehan and other stories
The King of Hearts and other stories
Narcissus and other stories
Suleiman M. Nana – Biography

AHMED ESSOP

The Hajji
and other stories

PICADOR AFRICA

First published 1978 Ravan Press

This edition published
2004 by Picador Africa
an imprint of Pan Macmillan South Africa
P.O. Box 411717, Craighall, Johannesburg 2024
www.panmacmillan.co.za

ISBN 1 77010 005 9

© Copyright Ahmed Essop 1978

The right of Ahmed Essop to be identified as the
author of this work has been asserted by him in accordance
with the Copyright Act No 98 of 1978

All rights reserved. No part of this publication may be reproduced,
stored in or introduced into a retrieval system, or transmitted in any
form or by any means (electronic, mechanical, photocopying, recording,
or otherwise) without the prior written permission of the
publisher. Any person who does any unauthorised act in relation to this
publication may be liable for criminal prosecution and civil
claims for damages.

Typeset in 10 on 13pt Palatino by PH Setting
Cover design: Lionel McMurray
Cover photographs courtesy of Gallo Images

Printed and bound in South Africa by CTP Book Printers

For Farida

Contents

Foreword	ix
The Hajji	1
The Betrayal	16
The Yogi	22
Dolly	29
Two Sisters	32
Father and Son	39
Hajji Musa and the Hindu Fire-Walker	42
The Target	54
Aziz Khan	60
Gladiators	66
Black and White	72
The Commandment	76
Red Beard's Daughter	79
Film	83
Obsession	93
Gerty's Brother	98
Ten Years	104
In Two Worlds	109
Labyrinth	114
The Notice	119
In the Train	124
Mr Moonreddy	127

Foreword

STORIES BY AHMED ESSOP began to appear in magazines and anthologies from 1969. They revealed such talent and freshness of matter and outlook that readers soon began to look forward to the publication of an unusually attractive and important collection. I believe that *The Hajji and other Stories* fulfils these expectations completely.

The stories centre on the vivid aromatic world of Johannesburg's Indian community in Fordsburg, with its unique blend of religious, political, cultural and economic preoccupations. This is not to suggest that the interest is defined by a racial line. Characters of every South African extraction occur in Ahmed Essop's pages, and this is merely one element in a pattern of contrasts based on age, temperament, income, education and above all occupation – among others, waiters, philosophers and shopkeepers, housewives, journalists, gangsters and soldiers, tarts, servants and mystics, a government inspector and a Molvi find rôles in these stories.

Nor does Essop's intimate involvement with Fordsburg confine the stories to that one place. It would be more accurate to describe his world as comprehending everything that oriental Fordsburg impinges on and overflows into. He thus adds a new world to those already represented in South African fiction. With nothing more to commend it this book would take a notable place in our literature.

But there is a great deal more to commend it. Ahmed Essop is a natural master of the story-teller's art with a fine feeling for situation, character and atmosphere. Though never evasive where the harsh social realities of his chosen scene are concerned, his writing is gentle and balanced in spirit, with humour and compassion bringing various levels of comedy and tragedy into his scope. This emotional richness, as well as the vivacious variety of his scene, is reminiscent of V.S. Naipaul whose fiction Essop admires. But among South African writers, it is hard to think of another, aside from Bosman, who is capable of bringing off, on the one hand, stories as lightheartedly funny as 'Hajji Musa and the Hindu Fire-Walker', as sweepingly satirical as 'Film' and, on the other, ones as astringently poignant as 'Gerty's Brother', as mysteriously disturbing as 'Mr Moonreddy', as poetically sombre as 'The Hajji'.

Perhaps even more impressive than the range of the emotional chords struck is the subtle combination of feelings within many of the stories. By the time we reach the end, for example, of 'Gladiators', 'Two Sisters', 'Obsession' or 'Ten Years', we experience such an interweaving of contrary sympathies that we might be contemplating our own fallible selves rather than characters in stories.

Yet nothing is technically forced or intellectually strained. On the contrary, Essop's style and approach, apart from the appropriate stiffening of a slightly formal manner, are as simple and direct as possible. His subtlety is born out of nothing more nor less than his fascination with the endlessly varied ways of the human heart. Thence the power to amuse, delight, move and challenge us. Thence an achievement of a timeless sort.

Lionel Abrahams

The Hajji

WHEN THE TELEPHONE RANG several times one evening and his wife did not attend to it as she usually did, Hajji Hassen, seated on a settee in the lounge, cross-legged and sipping tea, shouted: 'Salima, are you deaf?' And when he received no response from his wife and the jarring bell went on ringing, he shouted again: 'Salima, what's happened to you?'

The telephone stopped ringing. Hajji Hassen frowned in a contemplative manner, wondering where his wife was now. Since his return from Mecca after the pilgrimage, he had discovered novel inadequacies in her, or perhaps saw the old ones in a more revealing light. One of her salient inadequacies was never to be around when he wanted her. She was either across the road confabulating with her sister, or gossiping with the neighbours, or away on a shopping spree. And now, when the telephone had gone on assaulting his ears, she was not in the house. He took another sip of the strongly spiced tea to stifle the irritation within him.

When he heard the kitchen door open he knew that Salima had entered. The telephone burst out again in a metallic shrill and the Hajji shouted for his wife. She hurried to the phone.

'Hullo … Yes … Hassen … Speak to him? … Who speaking? … Caterine? … Who Caterine? … Au-right … I call him.'

She put the receiver down gingerly and informed her husband in Gujarati that a woman named 'Caterine' wanted to speak to him. The name evoked no immediate association in his memory. He descended from the settee and squeezing his feet into a pair of crimson sandals, went to the telephone.

'Hullo … Who? … Catherine? … No, I don't know you … Yes … Yes … Oh … now I remember … Yes … '

He listened intently to the voice, urgent, supplicating. Then he gave his answer:

'I am afraid I can't help him. Let the Christians bury him. His last wish means nothing to me … Madam, it's impossible …

No ... Let him die ... Brother? Pig! Pig! Bastard!' He banged the receiver onto the telephone in explosive annoyance.

'O Allah!' Salima exclaimed. 'What words! What is this all about?'

He did not answer but returned to the settee, and she quietly went to the bedroom.

Salima went to bed and it was almost midnight when her husband came into the room. His earlier vexation had now given place to gloom. He told her of his brother Karim who lay dying in Hillbrow. Karim had cut himself off from his family and friends ten years ago; he had crossed the colour line (his fair complexion and grey eyes serving as passports) and gone to cohabit with a white woman. And now that he was on the verge of death he wished to return to the world he had forsaken and to be buried under Moslem funeral rites and in a Moslem cemetery.

Hajji Hassen had, of course, rejected the plea, and for good reason. When his brother had crossed the colour line, he had severed his family ties. The Hajji at that time had felt excoriating humiliation. By going over to the white Herrenvolk, his brother had trampled on something that was vitally part of him, his dignity and self-respect. But the rejection of his brother's plea involved a straining of the heartstrings and the Hajji did not feel happy. He had recently sought God's pardon for his sins in Mecca, and now this business of his brother's final earthly wish and his own intransigence was in some way staining his spirit.

The next day Hassen rose at five to go to the mosque. When he stepped out of his house in Newtown the street lights were beginning to pale and clusters of houses to assume definition. The atmosphere was fresh and heady, and he took a few deep breaths. The first trams were beginning to pass through Bree Street and were clanging along like decrepit yet burning spectres towards the Johannesburg City Hall. Here and there a figure moved along hurriedly. The Hindu fruit and vegetable hawkers were starting up their old trucks in the yards, preparing to go out for the day to sell to suburban housewives.

When he reached the mosque the Somali muezzin in the ivory-domed minaret began to intone the call for prayers. After prayers, he remained behind to read the Koran in the company of two other men. When he had done the sun was shining brilliantly in the courtyard onto the flowers and the fountain with its goldfish.

Outside the house he saw a car. Salima opened the door and whispered, 'Caterine'. For a moment he felt irritated, but realising that he might as well face her he stepped boldly into the lounge.

Catherine was a small woman with firm fleshy legs. She was seated cross-legged on the settee, smoking a cigarette. Her face was almost boyish, a look that partly originated in her auburn hair which was cut very short, and partly in the smallness of her head. Her eye-brows, firmly pencilled, accentuated the grey-green glitter of her eyes. She was dressed in a dark grey costume.

He nodded his head at her to signify that he knew who she was. Over the telephone he had spoken with aggressive authority. Now, in the presence of the woman herself, he felt a weakening of his masculine fibre.

'You must, Mr Hassen, come to see your brother.'

'I am afraid I am unable to help,' he said in a tentative tone. He felt uncomfortable; there was something so positive and intrepid about her appearance.

'He wants to see you. It's his final wish.'

'I have not seen him for ten years.'

'Time can't wipe out the fact that he's your brother.'

'He is a white. We live in different worlds.'

'But you must see him.'

There was a moment of strained silence.

'Please understand that he's not to blame for having broken with you. I am to blame. I got him to break with you. Really you must blame me, not Karim.'

Hassen found himself unable to say anything. The thought that she could in some way have been responsible for his brother's rejection of him had never occurred to him. He looked at his feet in awkward silence. He could only state in a lazily recalcitrant tone: 'It is not easy for me to see him.'

'Please come Mr Hassen, for my sake, please. I'll never be able to bear it if Karim dies unhappily. Can't you find it in your heart to forgive him, and to forgive me?'

He could not look at her. A sob escaped from her, and he heard her opening her handbag for a handkerchief.

'He's dying. He wants to see you for the last time.'

Hassen softened. He was overcome by the argument that she had been responsible for taking Karim away. He could hardly look on her responsibility as being in any way culpable. She was a woman.

'If you remember the days of your youth, the time you spent together with Karim before I came to separate him from you, it will be easier for you to pardon him.'

Hassen was silent.

'Please understand that I am not a racialist. You know the conditions in this country.'

He thought for a moment and then said: 'I will go with you.'

He excused himself and went to his room to change. After a while they set off for Hillbrow in her car.

He sat beside her. The closeness of her presence, the perfume she exuded stirred currents of feeling within him. He glanced at her several times, watched the deft movements of her hands and legs as she controlled the car. Her powdered profile, the outline taut with a resolute quality, aroused his imagination. There was something so businesslike in her attitude and bearing, so involved in reality (at the back of his mind there was Salima, flaccid, cow-like and inadequate) that he could hardly refrain from expressing his admiration.

'You must understand that I'm only going to see my brother because you have come to me. For no one else would I have changed my mind.'

'Yes, I understand. I'm very grateful.'

'My friends and relatives are going to accuse me of softness, of weakness.'

'Don't think of them now. You have decided to be kind to me.'

The realism and the commonsense of the woman's words! He was overwhelmed by her.

The car stopped at the entrance of a building in Hillbrow. They took the lift. On the second floor three white youths entered and were surprised at seeing Hassen. There was a separate lift for non-whites. They squeezed themselves into a corner, one actually turning his head away with a grunt of disgust. The lift reached the fifth floor too soon for Hassen to give a thought to the attitude of the three white boys. Catherine led him to apartment 65.

He stepped into the lounge. Everything seemed to be carefully arranged. There was her personal touch about the furniture, the ornaments, the paintings. She went to the bedroom, then returned and asked him in.

Karim lay in bed, pale, emaciated, his eyes closed. For a moment Hassen failed to recognize him: ten years divided them. Catherine placed a chair next to the bed for him. He looked at his brother and again saw, through ravages of illness, the familiar features. She sat on the bed and rubbed Karim's hands to wake him. After a while he began to show signs of consciousness. She called him tenderly by his name. When he opened his eyes he did not recognize the man beside him, but by degrees, after she had repeated Hassen's name several times, he seemed to understand. He stretched out a hand and Hassen took it, moist and repellent. Nausea swept over him, but he could not withdraw his hand as his brother clutched it firmly.

'Brother Hassen, please take me away from here.'

Hassen's agreement brought a smile to his lips.

Catherine suggested that she drive Hassen back to Newtown where he could make preparations to transfer Karim to his home.

'No, you stay here. I will take a taxi.' And he left the apartment.

In the corridor he pressed the button for the lift. He watched the indicator numbers succeeding each other rapidly, then stop at five. The doors opened – and there they were again, the three white youths. He hesitated. The boys looked at him tauntingly. Then suddenly they burst into deliberately brutish laughter.

'Come into the parlour,' one of them said.

'Come into the Indian parlour,' another said in a cloyingly mocking voice.

Hassen looked at them, annoyed, hurt. Then something snapped within him and he stood there, transfixed. They laughed at him in a raucous chorus as the lift doors shut.

He remained immobile, his dignity clawed. Was there anything so vile in him that the youths found it necessary to maul that recess of self-respect within him? 'They are whites,' he said to himself in bitter justification of their attitude.

He would take the stairs and walk down the five floors. As he descended he thought of Karim. Because of him he had come there and because of him he had been insulted. The enormity of the insult bridged the gap of ten years when Karim had spurned him, and diminished his being. Now he was diminished again.

He was hardly aware that he had gone down five floors when he reached ground level. He stood still, expecting to see the three youths again. But the foyer was empty and he could see the reassuring activity of street life through the glass panels. He quickly walked out as though he would regain in the hubbub of the street something of his assaulted dignity.

He walked on, structures of concrete and glass on either side of him, and it did not even occur to him to take a taxi. It was in Hillbrow that Karim had lived with the white woman and forgotten the existence of his brother; and now that he was dying he had sent for him. For ten years Karim had lived without him. O Karim! The thought of the youth he had loved so much during the days they had been together at the Islamic Institute, a religious seminary though it was governed like a penitentiary, brought the tears to his eyes and he stopped against a shop-window and wept. A few pedestrians looked at him. When the shopkeeper came outside to see the weeping man, Hassen, ashamed of himself, wiped his eyes and walked on.

He regretted his pliability in the presence of the white woman. She had come unexpectedly and had disarmed him with her presence and subtle talk. A painful lump rose in his throat as he set his heart against forgiving Karim. If his brother had had no personal dignity in sheltering behind his white skin, trying to be what he was not, he was not going to allow his own moral worth to be depreciated in any way.

When he reached central Johannesburg he went to the station and took the train. In the coach with the blacks he felt at ease and regained his self-possession. He was among familiar faces, among people who respected him. He felt as though he had been spirited away by a perfumed well-made wax doll, but had managed with a prodigious effort to shake her off.

When he reached home Salima asked him what had been decided and he answered curtly, 'Nothing.' But feeling elated after his escape from Hillbrow he added condescendingly, 'Karim left of his own accord. We should have nothing to do with him.'

Salima was puzzled, but she went on preparing supper.

Catherine received no word from Hassen and she phoned him. She was stunned when he said; 'I'm sorry but I am unable to offer any help.'

'But ... '

'I regret it. I made a mistake. Please make some other arrangements. Goodbye.'

With an effort of will he banished Karim from his mind. Finding his composure again he enjoyed his evening meal, read the paper and then retired to bed. Next morning he went to mosque as usual, but when he returned home he found Catherine there again. Angry that she should have come, he blurted out: 'Listen to me, Catherine. I can't forgive him. For ten years he didn't care about me, whether I was alive or dead. Karim means nothing to me now.'

'Why have you changed your mind? Do you find it so difficult to forgive him?'

'Don't talk to me of forgiveness. What forgiveness, when he threw me aside and chose to go with you? Let his white friends see to him, let Hillbrow see to him.'

'Please, please, Mr Hassen, I beg you ... '

'No, don't come here with your begging. Please go away.'

He opened the door and went out. Catherine burst into tears. Salima comforted her as best she could.

'Don't cry Caterine. All men hard. Dey don't understand.'

'What shall I do now?' Catherine said in a defeated tone. She was an alien in the world of the non-whites. 'Is there no one who can help me?'

'Yes, Mr Mia help you,' replied Salima.

In her eagerness to find some help, she hastily moved to the door. Salima followed her and from the porch of her home directed her to Mr Mia's. He lived in a flat on the first floor of an old building. She knocked and waited in trepidation.

Mr Mia opened the door, smiled affably and asked her in.

'Come inside, lady; sit down ... Fatima,' he called to his daughter, 'bring some tea.'

Mr Mia was a man in his fifties, his bronze complexion partly covered by a neatly trimmed beard. He was a well-known figure in the Indian community. Catherine told him of Karim and her abortive appeal to his brother. Mr Mia asked one or two questions, pondered for a while and then said: 'Don't worry, my good woman. I'll speak to Hassen. I'll never allow a Muslim brother to be abandoned.'

Catherine began to weep.

'Here, drink some tea and you'll feel better.' He poured tea. Before Catherine left he promised that he would phone her that evening and told her to get in touch with him immediately should Karim's condition deteriorate.

Mr Mia, in the company of the priest of the Newtown mosque, went to Hassen's house that evening. They found several relatives of Hassen's seated in the lounge (Salima had spread the word of Karim's illness). But Hassen refused to listen to their pleas that Karim should be brought to Newtown.

'Listen to me Hajji,' Mr Mia said. 'Your brother can't be allowed to die among the Christians.'

'For ten years he has been among them.'

'That means nothing. He's still a Muslim.'

The priest now gave his opinion. Although Karim had left the community, he was still a Muslim. He had never rejected the religion and espoused Christianity, and in the absence of any evidence to the contrary it had to be accepted that he was a Muslim brother.

'But for ten years he has lived in sin in Hillbrow.'

'If he has lived in sin that is not for us to judge.'

'Hajji, what sort of a man are you? Have you no feeling for your brother?' Mr Mia asked.

'Don't talk to me about feeling. What feeling had he for me when he went to live among the whites, when he turned his back on me?'

'Hajji, can't you forgive him? You were recently in Mecca.'

This hurt Hassen and he winced. Salima came to his rescue with refreshments for the guests.

The ritual of tea-drinking established a mood of conviviality and Karim was forgotten for a while. After tea they again tried to press Hassen into forgiving his brother, but he remained adamant. He could not now face Catherine without looking ridiculous. Besides he felt integrated now; he would resist anything that negated him.

Mr Mia and the priest departed. They decided to raise the matter with the congregation in the mosque. But they failed to move Hassen. Actually his resistance grew in inverse ratio as more people came to learn of the dying Karim and Hassen's refusal to forgive him. By giving in he would be displaying mental dithering of the worst kind, as though he were a man without an inner fibre, decision and firmness of will.

Mr Mia next summoned a meeting of various religious dignitaries and received their mandate to transfer Karim to Newtown without his brother's consent. Karim's relatives would be asked to care for him, but if they refused Mr Mia would take charge.

The relatives, not wanting to offend Hassen and also feeling that Karim was not their responsibility, refused.

Mr Mia phoned Catherine and informed her of what had been decided. She agreed that it was best for Karim to be amongst his people during his last days. So Karim was brought to Newtown in an ambulance hired from a private nursing home and housed in a little room in a quiet yard behind the mosque.

The arrival of Karim placed Hassen in a difficult situation and he bitterly regretted his decision not to accept him into his own home. He first heard of his brother's arrival during the morning prayers when the priest offered a special prayer for the recovery of the sick man. Hassen found himself in the curious position of being forced to pray for his brother. After prayers several people went to see the sick man, others went up to Mr Mia to offer help. Hassen felt out of place and as soon as the opportunity presented itself he slipped out of the mosque.

In a mood of intense bitterness, scorn for himself, hatred of those who had decided to become his brother's keepers, infinite hatred for Karim, Hassen went home. Salima sensed her husband's mood and did not say a word to him.

In his room he debated with himself. In what way should he conduct himself so that his dignity remained intact? How was he to face the congregation, the people in the streets, his neighbours? Everyone would soon know of Karim and smile at him half sadly, half ironically, for having placed himself in such a ridiculous position. Should he now forgive the dying man and transfer him to his home? People would laugh at him, snigger at his cowardice, and Mr Mia perhaps even deny him the privilege: Karim was now *his* responsibility. And what would Catherine think of him? Should he go away somewhere (on the pretext of a holiday) to Cape Town, to Durban? But no, there was the stigma of being called a renegade. And besides, Karim might take months to die, he might not die at all.

'O Karim, why did you have to do this to me?' he said, moving towards the window and drumming at the pane nervously. It galled him that a weak, dying man could bring such pain to him.

An adversary could be faced, one could either vanquish him or be vanquished, with one's dignity unravished, but with Karim what could he do?

He paced his room. He looked at his watch; the time for afternoon prayers was approaching. Should he expose himself to the congregation? 'O Karim! Karim!' he cried, holding on to the burglar-proof bar of his bedroom window. Was it for this that he had made the pilgrimage – to cleanse his soul in order to return into the penumbra of sin? If only Karim would die he would be relieved of his agony. But what if he lingered on? What if he recovered? Were not prayers being said for him? He went to the door and shouted in a raucous voice: 'Salima!'

But Salima was not in the house. He shouted again and again, and his voice echoed hollowly in the rooms. He rushed into the lounge, into the kitchen, he flung the door open and looked into the yard.

He drew the curtains and lay on his bed in the dark. Then he heard the patter of feet in the house. He jumped up and shouted for his wife. She came hurriedly.

'Salima, Salima, go to Karim, he is in a room in the mosque yard. See how he is, see if he is getting better. Quickly!'

Salima went out. But instead of going to the mosque, she entered her neighbour's house. She had already spent several hours sitting beside Karim. Mr Mia had been there as well as Catherine – who had wept.

After a while she returned from her neighbour. When she opened the door her husband ran to her. 'How is he? Is he very ill? Tell me quickly!'

'He is very ill. Why don't you go and see him?'

Suddenly, involuntarily, Hassen struck his wife in the face.

'Tell me, is he dead? Is he dead?' he screamed.

Salima cowered in fear. She had never seen her husband in this raging temper. What had taken possession of the man? She retired quickly to the kitchen. Hassen locked himself in the bedroom.

During the evening he heard voices. Salima came to tell him that several people, led by Mr Mia, wanted to speak to him urgently. His first impulse was to tell them to leave immediately; he was not prepared to meet them. But he had been wrestling with himself for so many hours that he welcomed a moment when he could be in the company of others. He stepped boldly into the lounge.

'Hajji Hassen,' Mr Mia began, 'please listen to us. Your brother has not long to live. The doctor has seen him. He may not outlive the night.'

'I can do nothing about that,' Hassen replied, in an audacious matter-of-fact tone that surprised him and shocked the group of people.

'That is in Allah's hand,' said the merchant Gardee. 'In our hands lie forgiveness and love. Come with us now and see him for the last time.'

'I cannot see him.'

'And what will it cost you?' asked the priest who wore a long black cloak that fell about his sandalled feet.

'It will cost me my dignity and my manhood.'

'My dear Hajji, what dignity and what manhood? What can you lose by speaking a few kind words to him on his death-bed? He was only a young man when he left.'

'I will do anything, but going to Karim is impossible.'

'But Allah is pleased by forgiveness,' said the merchant.

'I am sorry, but in my case the circumstances are different. I am indifferent to him and therefore there is no necessity for me to forgive him.'

'Hajji,' said Mr Mia, 'you are only indulging in glib talk and you know it. Karim is your responsibility, whatever his crime.'

'Gentlemen, please leave me alone.'

And they left. Hassen locked himself in his bedroom and began to pace the narrow space between bed, cupboard and wall. Suddenly, uncontrollably, a surge of grief for his dying brother welled up within him.

'Brother! Brother!' he cried, kneeling on the carpet beside his bed and smothering his face in the quilt. His memory unfolded a time when Karim had been ill at the Islamic Institute and he had cared for him and nursed him back to health. How much he had loved the handsome youth!

At about four in the morning he heard an urgent rapping. He left his room to open the front door.

'Brother Karim dead,' said Mustapha, the Somali muezzin of the mosque, and he cupped his hands and said a prayer in Arabic. He wore a black cloak and a white skull-cap. When he had done he turned and walked away.

Hassen closed the door and went out into the street. For a moment his release into the street gave him a feeling of sinister jubilation, and he laughed hysterically as he turned the corner and stood next to Jamal's fruit shop. Then he walked on. He wanted to get away as far as he could from Mr Mia and the priest who would be calling upon him to prepare for the funeral. That was no business of his. They had brought Karim to Newtown and they should see to him.

He went up Lovers' Walk and at the entrance of Orient House he saw the night-watchman sitting beside a brazier. He hastened up to him, warmed his hands by the fire, but he did this more as a gesture of fraternization as it was not cold, and he said a few words facetiously. Then he walked on.

His morbid joy was ephemeral, for the problem of facing the congregation at the mosque began to trouble him. What opinion would they have of him when he returned? Would they not say: he hated his brother so much that he forsook his prayers, but now that his brother is no longer alive he returns. What a man! What a Muslim!

When he reached Vinod's Photographic Studio he pressed his forehead against the neon-lit glass showcase and began to weep.

A car passed by filling the air with nauseous gas. He wiped his eyes, and looked for a moment at the photographs in the showcase; the relaxed, happy, anonymous faces stared at him, faces whose momentary expressions were trapped in film. Then he walked on. He passed a few shops and then reached Broadway Cinema where he stopped to look at the lurid posters. There were heroes, lusty, intrepid, blasting it out with guns; women in various stages of undress; horrid monsters from another planet plundering a city; Dracula.

Then he was among the quiet houses and an avenue of trees rustled softly. He stopped under a tree and leaned against the trunk. He envied the slumbering people in the houses around him, their freedom from the emotions that jarred him. He would not return home until the funeral of his brother was over.

When he reached the Main Reef Road the east was brightening up. The lights along the road seemed to be part of the general haze. The buildings on either side of him were beginning to thin and on his left he saw the ghostly mountains of mine sand. Dawn broke over the city and when he looked back he saw the silhouettes of tall buildings bruising the sky. Cars and trucks were now rushing past him.

He walked for several miles and then branched off onto a gravel road and continued for a mile. When he reached a clump of blue-gum trees he sat down on a rock in the shade of the trees. From where he sat he could see a constant stream of traffic flowing along the highway. He had a stick in his hand which he had picked up along the road, and with it he prodded a crevice in the rock. The action, subtly, touched a chord in his memory and he was sitting on a rock with Karim beside him. The rock was near a river that flowed a mile away from the Islamic Institute. It was a Sunday. He had a stick in his hand and he prodded at a crevice and the weather-worn rock flaked off and Karim was gathering the flakes.

'Karim! Karim!' he cried, prostrating himself on the rock, pushing his fingers into the hard roughness, unable to bear the death of that beautiful youth.

He jumped off the rock and began to run. He would return to Karim. A fervent longing to embrace his brother came over him, to touch that dear form before the soil claimed him. He ran until he was tired, then walked at a rapid pace. His whole existence precipitated itself into one motive, one desire, to embrace his brother in a final act of love.

His heart beating wildly, his hair dishevelled, he reached the highway and walked on as fast as he could. He longed to ask for a lift from a passing motorist but could not find the courage to look back and signal. Cars flashed past him, trucks roared in pain.

When he reached the outskirts of Johannesburg it was nearing ten o'clock. He hurried along, now and then breaking into a run. Once he tripped over a cable and fell. He tore his trousers in the fall and found his hands were bleeding. But he was hardly conscious of himself, wrapped up in his one purpose.

He reached Lovers' Walk, where cars growled around him angrily; he passed Broadway Cinema, rushed towards Orient House, turned the corner at Jamal's fruit shop. And stopped.

The green hearse, with the crescent moon and stars emblem, passed by; then several cars with mourners followed, bearded men, men with white skull-caps on their heads, looking rigidly ahead, like a procession of puppets, indifferent to his fate. No one saw him.

The Betrayal

WHEN DR KAMAL CLOSED HIS surgery door one Friday night, he felt that a door had closed on his past.

He was a tall slender man, mud-complexioned, with a balding cranium that gave him a distinguished scholarly appearance. He was not only a physician and a well-known politician, but a connoisseur and collector of works of art displaying the agony of the proletariat in fields and factories. His entire collection was on display in his gallery-cum-study at home. He had received his medical and political education in India; his ability at the game of cricket had also been developed in that country. He was a religious man and every Friday he would dutifully attend the mosque in Newtown to genuflect in prayer.

For days he had been enmeshed in a dilemma, which had originated when a new political group in Fordsburg proclaimed its inaugural meeting by means of notices stuck on walls and lampposts. The emergence of the group, mainly consisting of youth, posed a threat to the Orient Front of which Dr Kamal was the president. A successful public meeting could be the first stage in its growth into a powerful rival political body, a body that could in time eliminate the Orient Front as a representative organization. There was also a personal threat. Dr Kamal had achieved the presidency of the Orient Front after years of patient waiting and he was afraid that his position would lose some of its lustre with the appearance of another political body. He was also the political mentor of the Fordsburg youth and felt that his prestige and status would suffer a reduction if the new group drew deserters from the Youth League of which he was the founder. There was only one way to stop the threat: the new group had to be crushed at its inaugural meeting. But ... how was he to reconcile this action with the fact that he had been a professed disciple of Gandhi during his political life?

He drove in his small German car to the offices of the Orient Front in Park Road. At ten o'clock he was to address a clandestine meeting of members of the Youth League. He reached the building, parked his car at the entrance, and walked slowly up a flight of stairs.

Salim Rashid, chairman of the Youth League, was waiting for him.

'We are ready, Doc.'

'How many?'

'Forty-two.'

'Have you explained to them what they have to do?'

'Yes. You have only to say a few words to them.'

It had been Salim Rashid's idea that he should address the Youth League, after the doctor had discreetly suggested that the new political group should be annihilated, in accordance with the 'ethics of political survival', before it hatched something dangerous. Had he rejected the idea, Dr Kamal would have given Salim Rashid the impression that he was afraid. The young man's argument had been that a few words from their mentor, on the eve of the clash, would be sufficient to convince the members of the rightness of their action. In order to keep the doctor's role a secret he would arrange a nocturnal meeting.

Salim Rashid opened a door. It led into a large room with many chairs and several tables. Some members of the Youth League were talking in groups, others were outside on the balcony. There were portraits, rather crudely garish, of Gandhi on the walls.

'Friends, attention. Dr Kamal is here to address you.'

They settled down on the chairs. The doctor began:

'One of the most important duties of the Youth League – in fact it is part of its unwritten constitution – is to safeguard the integrity and retain the hegemony of its parent body the Orient Front, and prevent rival political organizations from trespassing on our traditional ground. You have a great responsibility towards the Indian people of this country. You cannot permit them to be divided. The despots will destroy us if we let this happen. Let me remind you that it has always been a thesis of mine that there is no essential conflict of principles between Gandhi and the Western political philosophers, that a violent revolt and a passive revolt are aspects of the dynamics of man's search for freedom.'

He paused for a moment, coughed into his clenched hand, and continued: 'You should always remember that you are not only a vital part of the Orient Front, but also the vanguard that must protect it from harm. Remember always that you have been chosen by history to shape the future of this country.'

Dr Kamal had done. The youths clapped their hands, then raised their fists and shouted a few belligerent slogans.

He left the premises immediately.

On his way home he decided to pass Gandhi Hall where the meeting was to be held the next day. His motive for passing by was rooted in a strange sudden notion that the new group too had decided to hold a secret nocturnal meeting. Fear inflamed the turbulence within him and he stopped his car, half-expecting to see a knot of people coming up the street to attend the meeting. But the street was deserted and the hall doors locked. A gust of wind rushed by, carrying with it a swarm of rasping papers. The irony of his role struck him with force. He, the professed disciple of Gandhi, had unleashed a demon that would profane the hall commemorative of the master's name.

He went home and locked himself in his study. This room had been the scene, in the early days when he had joined the Orient Front, of weekly lectures to the youth of Fordsburg under the title. 'A Study of the Dynamics of Political Action and Political Truth', which had gained such popularity that the numbers swelled and he had formed the Youth League. Its members had come to look upon him as their oracle on political matters. In his study he had expounded to them the political philosophy of the 'triumvirate', Marx, Lenin and Gandhi. He had spoken with veneration of Gandhi's passive resistance campaigns against the 'racist oligarchs' and had extolled him as a 'Titan in the history of humanity' as he had been the first to bring into the realm of politics the concepts of truth and non-violence. He had also proudly told the youth of his meetings with Gandhi while he was a medical student in India and his abandonment of radical and revolutionary ideas in politics.

When Dr Kamal took his seat in the hall he saw that it was packed with people. He felt his chest contract and he hurriedly lit a cigarette.

'Hullo, Doc,' said Rhada, the secretary of the Orient Front, sitting down beside him. 'Is our Youth League present?'

'This should be an interesting meeting,' he commented, pretending not to have heard the question.

'This should be their first and last meeting.'

Dr Kamal was jolted. So the secretary knew of the intentions of the Youth League? Salim Rashid had assured him that the plans were all secret and that he would not be implicated. Now someone had told the secretary – and perhaps many others – and though he seemed to approve of the planned disruption and violence there was no way of telling how he would react if things went wrong.

'There is Salim Rashid,' Rhada said, pointing towards the front.

'Yes,' Dr Kamal answered feebly.

'These upstarts can give us a lot of trouble if they are not stopped.'

'The youth must settle matters among themselves,' Dr Kamal said, with suppressed anger.

Several young men began adjusting the public address system on the stage and then one of them began to speak. He gave the audience a preliminary brief account of how he and several friends had been drawn to the politics of the People's Movement in Cape Town and had decided to form a branch in the city.

'Mr Chairman, I object!'

Salim Hoosein stood up.

'May I remind you that there is a political organization here, the Orient Front. You may have heard of it.'

'I have heard of it. But I feel that there is a need for a different kind of political organization. Let me explain … '

Several voices interjected:

'What do you mean?'

'Is the Front dead?'

'Are you issuing a challenge?'

The speaker pleaded for order and said that members of the audience would have ample time to ask questions later.

'Mr Chairman, are you trying to smear the Orient Front?' Salim Rashid shouted.

Before he could answer several voices accused the new group of trying to divide the Indian people in their liberatory struggle. Then someone boomed:

'Uncivilized Indians, don't you know anything about meeting procedure.'

Dr Kamal jumped up from his seat and turning in the direction of the voice said:

'I strongly object to the defamatory slur cast upon us by someone in the hall. For his information, I must state that we Indians are among the most civilized races of mankind, a people with a glorious culture ... '

'Well, that is quite plain to all,' a cynical voice near him said.

'Why don't you keep quiet and let the meeting get on?'

He sat down, his body quivering. The rebuke stung him with such ferocity that for a moment, while standing, he had felt his body reeling as if he was about to plunge down a vertiginous height. His dignity and status had suffered a humiliating reduction. What compelling force had made him jump up from his seat and expose himself to the audience and identify himself, so it seemed to him, with the opponents of the new political group? He had come as an observer – a delusion he had managed to sustain until a few moments ago – but now he had become involved in their dispute. He should have stayed at home. The new group seemed to have many more sympathizers than he had calculated; people were taking them seriously. If the Youth League was defeated ... he did not have time to complete the thought as, with the volume of the public address system amplified, the Chairman continued:

'Some of us felt that what we lacked here was a political body that would unify the oppressed. We are convinced that any organization opposed to racialism should not have a racial structure, such as that of the Orient Front, or the African Front ... '

Salim Rashid leapt from his seat.

'Don't insult the Orient Front! Don't insult the organization founded by the great Mahatma Gandhi!'

He rushed forward and immediately members of the Youth League rose to follow their leader. Friends and sympathizers of the new group in the audience, shocked at first by the sudden threat of violence, jumped up from their seats and pressed towards the front to join the fray.

There was uproar and panic. Women screamed. The stage became a mass of seething, pushing, wrestling, punching, shouting combatants. From the rear of the hall one had the impression that players in a drama were involved in a mock battle.

Someone ran out of the hall to telephone the police.

When Salim Rashid leapt from his seat shouting his battle cry and rushing forward, Dr Kamal had experienced a sharp conflict within. There was the urge to flee from the violence he had contrived, and there was a petrifying inertia compelling him to remain and witness the battle. He stayed, trapped by indecision and the ambiguity of his political commitment, but when he saw the opposition's determination to fight the Youth League members, he rose from his seat. He took a few hurried steps, reached the foyer and stopped at the door. Policemen with truncheons and guns rushed past him into the hall.

Driven by a turbid amalgam of curiosity, fear and bewilderment, Dr Kamal re-entered the hall and watched horrified at the new dimension added to the battle. Then he fled. The centre of his being that had been in turmoil during the past few weeks seemed to be undergoing a kind of physical rot and together with this feeling he sensed the approaching storm of reproach and stigma that would engulf him. He reached his car. As he drove homewards Salim Rashid's words – aroused flaming furies – pursued him:

'Don't insult our organization ... '

The Yogi

THE WISEST AND MOST LEARNED man in Fordsburg, many people said, was Yogi Khrishnasiva. His wisdom resided in an impenetrable deity-like silence; his learning was displayed by the volumes on philosophy, mysticism and Yoga that he always carried in his hands. His inscrutable silence led many people to believe that he was among the few devotees who had achieved union with Brahman.

There was a time when Yogi Khrishnasiva had been vocal. After completing his studies at the feet of a luminary in India he had returned to the country and toured its main cities where he had lectured to various groups and organizations. To that period belonged a number of mystical maxims (constituting the themes of his lectures) that enjoyed a brief vogue, maxims such as: non-being is life, being is death; man's life on earth is a phantasmagoric trek to nowhere; meat-eating is the root of all evil; if you have inner liberty, political liberty is unnecessary. He had had them printed on art paper with an elaborate border of Hindu deities and had issued the scrolls to individuals and groups. However, the Orient Front failed to be impressed and returned the scroll with a note saying that the Yogi was 'undermining the political struggle' and that he was 'nothing other than a stooge of the ruling class'.

The Yogi lived with his widowed mother in Orient Mansions, an apartment block in Terrace Road. He was a small meticulous person. He could not have weighed more than a hundred pounds. There was something alert and agile about his dark, neatly-groomed face, despite the quietness that pervaded his general appearance. He was always fashionably dressed and never appeared in the traditional robes worn by mystics. As the Yogi had inherited a fortune, he did no work. His life was devoted to Yoga and the occult.

One day several youths were gathered in Mr Das Patel's café – ternally smelling of sweetmeats, sub-tropical fruit and spiced delicacies – on the ground floor of Orient Mansions. Nazeem mentioned that he had heard that Yogi Khrishnasiva had been appointed a marriage guidance counsellor by a social welfare society.

'They could not have made a better choice,' commented the law student Soma. 'From his lofty moral and intellectual position he can survey the field of human follies and offer his wisdom.'

'Nonsense!' said Ebrahim – tall, curly-haired, dark – the political pundit. Sensing a verbal battle between the two everyone gathered around them.

'What does the Yogi, a bachelor, know about the problems of marriage?'

'Is it necessary for one to be married before one can say anything about marriage?'

'Tell me Soma, what does the Yogi, an ascetic, know about sex?'

Soma did not reply.

'Or take a parallel example. Can one give an account of life in a fascist dictatorship without actual experience?'

'Of course one can. In a democracy there will be a legal code; in a fascist dictatorship the individual will have no legal rights.'

'Do you seriously believe that anyone outside this country can have adequate knowledge of conditions here?'

'He can read about them, surely.'

'Certainly, but his knowledge will be academic.'

Soma took off his spectacles and wiped them with a handkerchief. The argument was stoking up but it was veering away from the Yogi and Mr Das Patel brought them back to him.

'You talk of Yogi Khrishnasiva and now you talk of dictatorship … Talk of Yogi and I say he fraud.'

Fraud! The word jolted them.

'I tell you he fraud. You boys too young to know.'

'Tell us! Tell us!' they chorused.

But Mr Das Patel was as inscrutable as the Yogi.

'Don' worry boys. I say he fraud, big fraud. I not Das Patel for nutting. One day you see. At moment I say nutting furder.'

'This is defamation of character,' Soma asserted.

'Defamation of who character? The Yogi? He got no character, my dear man.'

Everyone laughed.

'I say it is libellous to accuse a man without evidence.'

'Look here Soma, I not like you lawyers. You talk like old women in court and tell all Dick and Harry how clever you are. I know what I talking when I say the Yogi he fraud. Some day you see me right. Dat all.'

'You are accusing a man who practises renunciation. Who will believe you?'

'Renun … my foot! He practise renun … ? I not born yesterday. You tell your fader he practise renun … , not me.'

'Soma, shut up! Shut up!' several voices shot in. They pacified Mr Das Patel. He relented a little.

'I say he sleep wit wite women. One day you see me right. Dat all.'

After giving them this fresh jolt, Mr Das Patel refused to say anything further.

Someone who had gone out came back into the café to say that the Yogi was approaching. They hurried outside. As the Yogi passed by Mr Das Patel said loudly: 'He practise Yoga in bed.' Everyone burst into laughter. The Yogi, unshaken, went towards the entrance of Orient Mansions and climbed the stairs.

After several months Mr Das Patel's café was the arena of excitement. In the evening newspaper appeared the following item:

An Indian, Mr Indra Khrishnasiva (45), was arrested at 3 a.m. today outside a block of flats in President Street and charged under the Immorality Act. A white woman has also been taken into custody.

'I tell you boys, didn't I?' Mr Das Patel said. 'I tell you dat Yogi he fraud. He only Yogi to cheat wite women to sleep wit him. I tell you he no like black women. He black but he don' like black. He like wite goose meat!'

And he laughed animatedly.

'I know Yogi Khrishnasiva dese many years. But he never come into my shop. He don' smoke, he don' drink, he don' eat, he only ... ' Mr Das Patel's wife entered the café and the word remained unuttered. When she left he burst into a wild guffaw.

'He marrich counsellor! He marrich counsellor! He counsel well dat I can tell you boys. Husban' not giving sateesfaction, dan do dis. Dan he give demonstration.'

'Yes,' said Aziz Khan, the writer on Islam, who had come in to buy the newspaper. 'Under the guise of Yoga he practised his abominations ... '

'Practical Yoga,' Nazeem suggested and the shop rang with laughter.

Soma, who was not amused by the levity regarding the Yogi's arrest, now decided to examine the legal implications.

'I think the Yogi can be got off. It is not easy to catch people in the very act, for obviously anyone indulging in the act takes all the necessary precautions against prying eyes. Then again, in his case, the state has to prove his guilt. The rule that the accused is innocent until found guilty applies. This rule of course does not apply in cases of political crimes ... '

'Verbosity is a crime here ... ' Ebrahim interrupted.

'I think the Yogi will be set free because of his unimpeachable character. His lawyer need only bring witnesses ... '

'He go free like hell. Dey put him away in jail to become real Yogi.'

Everyone laughed.

'The Yogi belongs to a dead civilization,' Ebrahim said. 'In an era when politics governs everything, he turns his face towards the negatives of renunciation and asceticism ... attitudes which are essentially irresponsible.'

'Very high-falutin',' Mr Das Patel said, 'but the plain fact is he fraud, total fraud.'

The Yogi's case came up three days later and people flocked to the Magistrate's Court to listen to the proceedings. School pupils played truant, students at university decided not to attend lectures, Mr Das Patel left his wife to manage the café.

The seating accommodation in the court-room was divided – one section for Europeans and the other for Non-Europeans. In the European section there were six people, two women and four men. The Non-European section was crowded and many people stood in the corridors outside the court room.

The Yogi's face looked strained when he and the woman were brought into the court. The woman was frail in appearance, though her face was pretty. Her hair was light brown in colour and cut very short. She was neatly dressed in a blue costume.

The prosecutor opened the case by presenting the state's evidence against the Yogi and Miss Weston. He said that the police had received information that several white women were frequenting an apartment block in President Street. They decided to investigate. They came to know of the 'Ganges Society' and the premises they occupied in the building. They kept a watch on the activities of members of the society. One night a police patrol observed a woman entering the building. It waited till three in the morning and when the woman and the Yogi emerged from the building they were arrested.

The prosecutor then called several witnesses, and after handing in the report of the physician who had examined the couple immediately after arrest, closed the state's case. Counsels for the Yogi and Miss West-on had entered pleas of guilty on behalf of their clients, and now prepared for cross-examination in mitigation of punishment.

Miss Weston was called into the witness box. She told the court that being a novice she had placed her confidence in the Yogi and that he had seduced her. She was then questioned by her counsel.

'Miss Weston, you have stated that at the time of seduction you were naked. Does the practice of Yoga require the removal of clothing?'

'The guru suggested that I remove my clothing.'

'Did he give a reason?'

'He said that all clothing contaminated the body and prevented the divine spirit from finding liberation.'

'What happened after that?'

'The guru asked me to perform the posture called "Prana".'

'Please explain.'

'He told me to lie flat on my back, cross my legs below me, interlock my fingers on my navel, and meditate on the significance of sexual congress.'

Cross-examined by the Yogi's counsel, Miss Weston denied that she had removed her clothing in order to sexually entice the Yogi.

The Yogi was next called to give evidence.

'Does the performance of Yoga require the removal of some clothing?'

'Yes.'

'What garments did Miss Weston remove?'

'She removed her skirt, blouse and slip. She said her brassiere was too tight and she removed it.'

'Anything else?'

The Yogi hesitated before answering.

'She removed her intimate garment.'

'Did you suggest that she remove it?'

'No.'

'Do you think that the removal of the garment was a deliberate act of provocation and enticement?'

'Yes, positively.'

The Yogi was then cross-examined by Miss Weston's counsel. To the assertion that he had misused Yoga and mysticism to seduce the lady, he answered:

'I repudiate that suggestion. I am an ascetic. All yogis are ascetics.'

'Yogi Khrishnasiva, is the presence of a naked woman an impediment to the liberation of the divine spirit in man, or is she an incentive?'

He did not answer immediately. He smiled in self-confidence and then answered:

'A naked woman is neither an impediment nor an incentive.'

'Could you explain that?'

The Yogi smiled again.

'We Yogis are indifferent to the state of the human body, whether in a state of dress or undress.'

'Do you think that it is seemly to perform various sacred exercises without any clothing?'

'My previous premise answers this question.'

'Why did you not ask Miss Weston to dress even if she had undressed of her own accord?'

'My previous premise answers this question as well.'

The lawyer paused for a moment and then said:

'Yogi Khrishnasiva, in your evidence you stated that you were enticed. Did you mean by that that you made the first advances?'

'She made the first advances.'

'And you succumbed?'

'I was enticed. I was overpowered.'

'But you have also spoken of the indifference of the Yogi in the presence of a naked woman?'

The Yogi remained silent.

'So you cannot maintain you were indifferent?'

'No,' he answered feebly.

'Then I suggest that you fraudulently employed the principles and practices of Yoga to seduce Miss Weston.'

The Yogi did not answer.

That evening the proceedings in court were a subject of discussion in Mr Das Patel's café. There was a report of the trial in the newspaper and a photograph of Miss Weston and the Yogi, but the Yogi's face was partly covered with his hand. Mr Das Patel was in a state of wild excitement. He parodied the cross-examination of the Yogi and his café resounded with laughter.

The next day, before judgment was delivered, the Yogi asked if he could make a statement. He began: 'Your worship, I wish to place on record that I object to this witch-hunt into the affairs of my private life … ' But the magistrate interrupted him with the rebuke that the court was not a forum for political speeches.

Dolly

'IF ANY OF YOU RICH INDIAN bastards try to joll my wife I will put a knife into your guts. What you know is to show off, talk big, ride in your big cars ... '

That was Dolly (Dooly) speaking in one of his violent, dangerous moods to bearded Mr Darsot, the spice and grain merchant. Mr Darsot dreaded meeting Dolly in the street. Yet when Dolly's scurrilities against Indians exploded, he could hardly move away, fearing a loss of dignity in ignominious retreat. Nor could he utter a word in defence, fearing to rouse Dolly's temper further. Trapped by his self-esteem and feebleness, he would listen to Dolly's unsavoury oratory:

'You Indian dogs, there were not enough bitches in India so you came to South Africa. Now you look for our wives. You lock your wives up and want to joll ours. Bring your wife here. I will show you, you Indian bastard ... '

Dolly would go on in this vein until he tired, or one of his friends pulled him away. Mr Darsot, displaying a tepid smile in moral victory, would hurry to seek refuge in his mansion, happy in the knowledge that he was physically unscathed.

Dolly was a small very dark man, athletic and wiry in build, and extraordinarily tough. I once saw two burly policemen vainly trying to pull him away from a railing to which he clung – and he only released his grip when one of them crushed his fingers with a brick. His black hair was always liberally oiled to combat its intractability. He was very ugly. His first wife had run away, unable to bear his inordinate jealousy and maniacal rages. His second wife Myrtle received a regular beating. There were times when he beat her so savagely that the police had to be called. At other times she was forced to go out with him and point out some lover (Myrtle felt that if her husband was jealous he might as well be justifiably jealous) somewhere in Fordsburg or Vrededorp. As they walked Dolly uttered menacing howls like some predacious animal. What ensued one would know after his return. If his revenge had been slaked he would shout coarsely: 'Indian swine, busted his guts, showed him what Dolly is made of, the bastard!' If thwarted, he would scream obscenities at everyone in the street and bang his fists against several doors, terrifying the people within.

Myrtle was a blowsy woman, tall, frizzy-haired, with thrusting buttocks. She believed in the attractiveness of her body and she flaunted it: one would see her sitting on a balustrade, her legs daringly outstretched; or bending over a tap in the yard, her raised skirt revealing the ample flesh of her legs; or dancing, her thighs and mons Veneris embalmed in tight-fitting slacks. She had two voices: an original voice, coarse and ebulliently vulgar, which one heard during bouts of altercation with her husband, or when she reviled some woman who dared to look at her 'as though I have taken your husband's you-know-what!' Her other voice was cloyingly euphonious, imitative of some woman's heard over the radio: 'Oh, you're a darling honey. You do look super today, don't you?' She was often abusively referred to by women as 'that Bushman bitch'.

One day Bibi arrived to board and lodge with Mrs Safi, the next-door neighbour of the Dollys. She caused a sensation the day she arrived. She was the most beautiful woman to set foot in our suburb. Black-haired and blue-eyed (she was the offspring of an Indian father and a Dutch mother) with a complexion like the white flower of the gardenia, her sylph-like beauty was at variance with the earthiness of our suburb.

Dolly was mesmerized by Bibi. He expressed his adoration to us in these terms: 'If any of you touch Bibi I will eat your livers.' One day she was hanging up some washing in the yard when she turned around and saw him. He was gazing at her in open-mouthed rapture from beside a tap, his dark face frothing with soap.

Dolly's behaviour underwent a transformation. He no longer roamed the street Caliban-like (though he drank and smoked marijuana as usual), nor involved himself in turbulent feuds with his wife. The presence of Bibi seemed to work like alchemy in him – he was seized with a sense of shame.

And Myrtle who had once inspired so much jealousy in him (jealousy which to her was a testimony of his love) and had weathered the storms of his sadistic rages, found herself cauterized by jealousy. She would scream uncouthly and accuse him of deceiving her with Bibi in a vain effort to trigger his natural turbulent response, but he remained placid. Her jealousy then found vent in threats against Bibi. She would speak coarsely, in the presence of other women: 'That half-caste bitch will not get away with it. Who does she think she is? Because she has a white skin and blue eyes she thinks she is someone great. One of these days I will get even with her.'

And she got 'even' with her. One day she waited for Bibi to arrive from work, grabbed her as she passed by her doorstep, and began assaulting her. Bibi screamed and various people rushed to her assistance. When I reached them Myrtle was in the grip of several strong hands. Bibi was cowering next to a wall, her clothes torn and her hair disarranged.

When Dolly came home someone told him of the assault on Bibi. He went next-door. He saw her bruised cheek, her inflamed eye, her nail-scratched neck.

That day hideous screams reverberated through the streets as Dolly, in a rampant mood, took Myrtle into the house and turned on her with his fists.

The police were called, but tired of the feud between man and wife stood around looking bored. We waited in the street. At last Myrtle stopped howling.

Dolly unlocked the door and saw Bibi amongst us. He burst into wild laughter.

'Beauty! Beauty! Come inside. She will never touch you again.'

He took Bibi by the hand and we followed them into the house.

Two Sisters

'When I want to baat den dey want to baat, when I want to go to lava-try den dey want to go also. Dey so shelfish in everything dey do. My stepmader and my fader dey jus lock demselves in de room, sometimes de whole day. I don't know wat dey do in dere. Dere is no food in de house and if dere is den we must cook. And den dey jus come out of dere room and eat all de food up.'

'Why didn't you speak to your father?'

'He don't listen to us since he marry dat woman. He very nice man, but when he marry dat woman all niceness disappear. She spoil him and he don't care for us anymore. Den I tell my sister Habiba we go away. Dat not true Habiba?'

'It true.'

'A friend tell us dere's room in dis yard. Dat's how we come here.'

Rookeya was talking to me and my friend Omar. The two sisters caused a sensation the day they arrived to live in the yard. They wore robe-like dresses with *ijars* (trousers). But there was nothing unusual in this. What was unusual was the colour of their hair. It was dyed blond. They looked rather odd as blond hair did not accord with Eastern features. They were both very hairy and waged a constant battle with the hair on their faces. 'Their hairiness,' my friend Omar said, 'indicates that they are sweet-time girls.' Rookeya was in her thirties and Habiba a few years younger.

Before long a change occurred in their mode of dress. Either because of some feminine quirk or the dictates of fashion the two sisters shed their Eastern garments (much to the consternation of Aziz Khan) and began to wear Western clothing.

Soon Omar and I were making love to the two sisters. I took the younger, Habiba. There was no real selection on our part: we gravitated towards them and indulged in some light-hearted lovemaking.

I found Habiba to be a woman who performed everything in jerks, as though her body were a wound-up mechanical toy. Her very walk was jerky and toy-like. She would look left, then right, and now and then look back as though fearing pursuit. Her arms would be bent almost at ninety-degree angles and she would tread the ground as though she were treading on a spike bed. When I kissed her I had the queer sensation that I was kissing a mobile skeleton.

After some time Omar and I tired of the company of the two sisters. Free of us they hitched themselves to other men.

In the morning one saw them emerge from their apartment, sprucely dressed, and descend the stairs, Rookeya always preceding Habiba protectively. They would go to Main Road and take the tram to their place of work. Both sisters worked as shop-assistants. They would return in the late afternoon, prepare food, eat, wash the dishes, and dress, sometimes in shimmering saris, and wait. Invariably men would come for them and they would be driven away in cars.

The attitude of the women in the yard towards the two sisters varied between frigid contempt and outright hostility. The married men in the yard, watched by their wives, were unable to approach them; but the unmarried ones fluttered around them despite Aziz Khan's prophecy that the 'two sisters and their lovers would go hand in hand into hell'.

On Saturday afternoons or Sunday mornings the two sisters, dressed in short pants or brief skirts, could be seen leaning on the iron balustrade of the balcony, talking to a group of young men gathered below, and laughing with them whenever anyone made a risque remark or cracked a joke.

And then, as anyone could have predicted, the two sisters were impregnated. At first they became alarmed and made random accusations. Omar was one of those charged by Rookeya as being responsible for her pregnancy.

She sent for me.

'Please tell Omar dat I pregnant and he fader of child. I marry him anytime. I frighten to tell him because he little bit young.'

'And how do you know?'
'We women we know who de fader. Is dat not so, Habiba?'
'It so.'
'Habiba, who is the father of your child?'
'He Hamid Majid of Newtown. He got shop.'
'And does he know?'
'I already tell him of baby, but he say he married and has six children. He say he look after baby.'
'You are lucky.'
'I also lucky,' Rookeya said, smiling.

I left to convey to Omar the allegation of paternity.

'How does that woman know that I made her pregnant?'
'Feminine intuition perhaps.'
'She thinks I am some stupid joker.'

Omar refused to face Rookeya. He feared that she might have some irrefutable evidence. What would his parents say? What would all the people say? Father of a harlot's child! He would be taunted by school children; his teachers would point him out as an example of degenerate youth.

After a few days he decided to face Rookeya and 'settle things' with her.

They quarrelled. There were 'tears, tantrums and hysterics' (according to Omar) but nothing was settled.

Rookeya sent for me again.

'Tell Omar it my baby. I make it and no man make it. Tell Omar I love him and he not worry.'
'But surely the child must have a father?'
'My child need no fader. It glad it has no fader, it tell me so. I feel it inside me, telling me so. My own fader not care for us, derefore my baby need no fader.'
'And Habiba?'
'Habiba also not worry about fader of baby. Dat not true, Habiba?'
'It true.'

And as the days passed the two sisters' wombs swelled. This provoked the anger and outraged the sense of morality of the people in the yard.

'Fine example they set our young girls,' said Mrs Musa to my landlady. 'Can't they see I have growing girls.'

'Lucky I got no girls to worry about.'

'I must tell my husband to do something. I cannot go on living alongside two pregnant unmarried women. And my eldest daughter is so friendly with them.'

Mrs Cassim, who was half-Chinese said: 'My mother used to tell me that in China unmarried girls never become pregnant.'

'Yes, that is true,' agreed Halima, the Malay woman. 'Even in Cape Town the women are better behaved. They go out with men but they behave themselves.'

'I wonder how they managed to get pregnant together,' said Mrs Cassim.

'Perhaps one man sleep with both during the same night,' suggested my landlady, and for a moment the seriousness of the discussion was forgotten in laughter.

'They practise polygamy,' said Dorothy, the builder Solomon's wife, trying to raise another laugh.

'I beg your pardon, Mrs Solomon,' Mrs Musa retorted, annoyed that her religion should be misunderstood. 'That is not polygamy. They are not married to one man.'

Hajji Fatima, who had been to Mecca the previous year, stated that in an Islamic country such as Arabia the two women would be stoned to death.

'They should cut off their pudenda,' said Dorothy (she was an avid reader of cheap novels), and although no one had heard the word before they understood what she meant. But it was something too bloody to contemplate. There was something more decent and clean in stoning.

While other women talked Aziz Khan's wife decided to act. One afternoon she glided out of her house, looked up at the apartment of the two sisters and stationed herself at the bottom of the stairs. Excitement flared through the yard and people gathered around her. When the two sisters arrived, she scrutinized their bulging bellies, spat and screamed:

'O Muslim women! O Muslim women! What have you done! What have you done! O Allah punish the women who call themselves Muslims and sin before you. O Muslims! O how you have fallen!'

And she fell down and wept. The two sisters looked at her in fear, hurried up the stairs and locked themselves in their apartment.

There was something so tragic in Mrs Khan's performance that gloom spread through the yard. Children were constantly reminded to keep quiet. People would emerge from their houses and look at the apartment of the two sisters as though something tragic was happening in there.

Aziz Khan, a whipcord lean man in over-sized clothing with the face of an overfed baby, said to us:

'If I had the time I would write a book on the nefarious activities of the two sisters. They pre-eminently exemplify the moral degeneration into which present-day Muslims are failing. They should be locked up in prison and starved to death.'

When someone suggested that they were not wholly responsible for their pregnancies, he answered:

'Are you suggesting that they were unable to guard their most sacred private places? Islam would never have attained its ineffable heights if it had allowed its daughters to run wild, to indulge in all sorts of acts of concupiscence.'

After a few months the two sisters gave birth to two girls.

There was much talk in the yard about the birth of the babies. Some felt sorry for the babies and wished to adopt them; others suggested that they be given to the carnivores in the zoo; others wanted to set fire to the apartment.

Aziz Khan felt that the time had come for action and that the two sisters and their babies should be 'ousted' from the yard. 'For their continued residence is a threat to the moral fibre of the people living in the yard and a blot on the fair name and fame of our religion and our holy Prophet.'

First he went to the gangster Gool, approaching him at his house immediately after noon prayers on Friday. But Gool, perhaps more interested in satisfying his hunger or finding moral talk odious, briskly disposed of him, shutting the door contemptuously.

His next call was on Molvi Haroon, priest at the Newtown mosque and head of the Islamic Academy. Abdulla, a disciple of Aziz Khan, accompanied him and gave us the following account of the interview:

'Aziz informed the Molvi of the serious moral problem facing us, and do you know what he said? He said that the punishment of the two women rested in the hands of Allah! Aziz, incensed at his cowardly fence-sitting, called him a 'stupid dwarf'. The Molvi grabbed his staff and Aziz thrust his left fist at him. I dragged Aziz out of the house.'

Aziz Khan's next call was on Mr Joosub, the landlord of the tenements in the yard. Mr Joosub was an eccentric who was always clad in koortah (white cotton smock), even on cold days. His head was always shaved and his beard bushy and long. He was obsessed by religion and would pray to Allah anywhere, even at street intersections. Once during the festival of Eid he came into the yard with a monkey. The monkey had a tasselled red fez strapped to its head. 'This monkey Muslim! This monkey Muslim!' he shouted to the spectators, especially directing his remarks to the servants. 'But you no Muslim, you no Muslim.' Then he scattered handfuls of coins – which turned out to be cents.

Mr Joosub expressed his willingness to oust the 'two bitches' from the yard. He would do so personally. He was king of several backyards in Fordsburg and would not tolerate the presence of 'bitches' on his domains.

He came one Sunday afternoon in his chauffeur-driven Mercedes. He stood at the foot of the stairs leading to the apartment of the two sisters and made several threatening pugilistic gestures. Excited people gathered around him. He struggled up the stairs, breathing hard and clutching the railing. When he reached the landing he paused to rest for a few minutes. The sisters were standing near the doorway. First he approached Rookeya and smacked her resoundingly on the cheek, shouting, 'Pig! Bitch! Pig!' in Gujarati. Habiba, who tried to escape past him, received a blow on the head. She fell and nearly came tumbling down the stairs. Mr Joosub then entered the apartment. The two sisters, shivering with fright, went towards the door to see what he would do next. Soon he appeared in the doorway, holding a primus stove in his hands, the brass contraption glinting in the sunlight, and he flung it over the railing. It fell with a clanging sound and several parts were shattered by the impact. Next a chair came hurtling down, followed by a pot and a bath. Other household articles followed in quick succession as the mania for destruction gripped Mr Joosub: crockery, linen, clothing. The two sisters, frightened, impotent, watched through the doorway as their landlord entered the apartment and gave way like marionettes as he emerged with some article.

Then, suddenly, Rookeya and Habiba screamed as Mr Joosub appeared in the doorway, holding one of the infants. They flung themselves on him. Mr Joosub tried to fend them off with one hand, while with the other he clutched the screaming infant.

At this stage Solomon made his way through the crowd and climbed the stairs. When he reached the landing he gently pushed the sisters aside, held Mr Joosub by the neck, shook him, took the infant and gave it to its mother, then gave Mr Joosub a hard push against the door frame so that his face bumped painfully against it. Retaining a firm hold of Mr Joosub he dragged him down the stairs. When they reached the ground the crowd gave way for them and the children burst into applause. Solomon conducted Mr Joosub to his Mercedes, opened the door and without any ceremony pushed him into the car. The chauffeur, knowing his cue, reversed the car out of the yard and drove off.

We didn't see Mr Joosub again for some time. But the sisters decided it was dangerous living in premises belonging to a madman. They found another apartment in Newtown and moved away.

Father and Son

SHORTLY AFTER THE TWO SISTERS LEFT, the premises they had occupied were renovated and expensively furnished. Everyone was eager to see the arrival of the new occupants. There was a rumour that Mr Joosub himself was coming to live in the yard in order to keep his tenants under surveillance, but the rumour proved false when one morning we saw a car enter the yard and from it emerge Mr Mayet the well-known jeweller and a young woman. Mr Mayet was over seventy years old. He wore an astrakhan fez and a newly-tailored suit. His beard was turning grey. He walked with a slight stoop and had to be assisted up the stairs by his chauffeur. The woman was tall and dusky in complexion. She was elegantly dressed in a white costume and her hair was elaborately coiffured. Her eyes were almond-shaped. She smiled at all those gazing at her.

Mr Mayet and the woman entered the apartment. The chauffeur carried in several portmanteaus and then left. The couple stayed in the apartment for the rest of that day and night. Before dawn on the next day, during the time of prayers at the mosque, Mr Mayet was seen leaving the yard.

The presence of the woman aroused a great deal of curiosity. Everyone wanted to see her, but she kept indoors. When she appeared on the balcony after a few days several people inquired of her who she was and where she came from. She told them that her name was Maimuna, that she came from Cape Town and that she was Mr Mayet's second wife.

There was much talk and gossip about Maimuna. There were those who were against her: her only motive for marrying an old man was to waste his money or inherit it. And there were those who were for her: the jeweller must have lured her with his money (or jewels) and tricked her family. Aziz Khan supported this view.

'There can be only one explanation for this mismatch of the century – the Malay woman's poor family must have been deceived into selling her to that doddering old idiot. There is just no depth to which the rich will not descend.'

When someone pointed out to him that he should not object as Mr Mayet was practising polygamy, he replied:

'Polygamy is a sacred religious institution and is not there for the moronic lust of the idle rich.'

A week later Aziz Khan issued a pamphlet entitled, 'Polygamy and Lust', but he avoided any reference to the jeweller.

Maimuna was a pleasant woman and she gained many friends. She entertained the women in her apartment, at first during the day and later at night as well when her husband began staying away every alternate night. Many women envied her. She was good-looking, had two servants, wore expensive clothes and jewellery and could telephone for a car at any time.

And then Asif arrived, entering the yard in a tangerine Alfa Romeo sports car. Asif was Mr Mayet's eldest son. He had been to England and had spent several years – largely unfruitful academically – at London University. He had come to meet his 'second mother'. He was slender, handsome, eternally wearing sun-glasses. He was never seen without a silk scarf around his neck and a cigarette in his mouth.

Asif began visiting Maimuna rather too often for the liking of some people and Myrtle declared that Asif was 'jolling his second mother'. The gossip-mongers were very excited and every time Asif's Alfa Romeo came into the yard they came out of their homes to look at him. Sometimes Asif came with his father and always helped him up the stairs. As time passed Asif's visits to his 'second mother' became more frequent and lasted many hours, so that his sports car looked like a permanent fixture in the yard.

Aziz Khan and his disciples were outraged at the 'highly immoral and objectionable behaviour of the black Englishman. Father and son delighting in the same cesspool!'

Not only did Asif spend much of his time with his 'second mother' in the apartment, but he began taking her out in his car, especially on the nights when his father stayed away.

'I have a good mind to phone Mr Mayet and tell him of his incestuous son of a goat fornicating with his mother,' Aziz Khan said to us.

Anyway, whether by Aziz Khan or someone else Mr Mayet came to know of the affair. He came one night when he was not expected and no sooner had he stepped out of his car than Asif's Alfa drove into the yard.

'You ape! You ape!' Mr Mayet shouted in Gujarati.

Father and son confronted each other. There was a terrible row. Mr Mayet disinherited his son in front of a crowd of people which had gathered to witness the spectacle. Asif answered back and dismissed his father as a 'rotten old tree'. People began to take sides and altercations broke out. Aziz Khan and several of his disciples attempted to attack Asif, others intervened, there was scuffling and shouting. In the melee several friends of Maimuna scratched Mr Mayet. Frightened at the commotion he had caused and fearing the arrival of the police, he quickly retreated to his car and was driven away by his chauffeur amid shouts of 'Coward!' and 'Serves you right!'

When peace returned Asif went away and Maimuna retired to her apartment.

The next day Asif arrived with two friends, but he did not come in his sports car. Maimuna telephoned her husband and told him to come to her immediately. She was sorry about the whole affair; she was innocent; he had been misinformed by jealous people. She had gone to the cinema; she had met Asif after the show and she had asked him to bring her home.

Mr Mayet came and when he knocked at the door Asif's friends opened it and one of them said:

'You are divorced.'

'Divorced? Who divorced me?'

'Maimuna. We are the witnesses.'

The people who had gathered below the stairs saw Mr Mayet step backwards.

'Asif, Asif,' he said several times and began to weep. Then he turned and walked down the stairs, helped by his chauffeur.

Hajji Musa and the Hindu Fire-Walker

'A̲ʟʟᴀʜ ʜᴀs sᴇɴᴛ me to you, Bibi Fatima.'

'Allah, Hajji Musa?'

'I assure you, Allah, my good lady. Listen to me carefully. There is something wrong with you. Either you have a sickness or there is an evil spell cast over your home. Can you claim that there is nothing wrong in your home, that your family is perfectly healthy and happy?'

'Well, Hajji Musa, you know my little Amir has a nasty cough that even Dr Kama! cannot cure and Soraya seems to have lost her appetite.'

'My good woman, you believe me now when I say Allah has sent me to you?'

Bibi Fatima's husband, Jogee, entered the room. Hajji Musa took no notice of him and began to recite (in Arabic) an extract from the Koran. When he had done he shook hands with Jogee.

'Listen to me, Bibi Fatima and brother Jogee. Sickness is not part of our nature, neither is it the work of our good Allah. It is the work of that great evil-doer Iblis, some people call him Satan. Well, I, by the grace of Allah,' (he recited another extract from the Koran) 'have been given the power to heal the sick and destroy evil. That is my work in life, even if I get no reward.'

'But Hajji Musa, you must live.'

'Bibi Fatima, Allah looks after me and my family. Now bring me two glasses of water and a candle.'

She hurried to the kitchen and brought the articles.

'Now bring me the children.'

'Jogee, please go and find Amir in the yard while I look for Soraya.'

Husband and wife went out. Meanwhile Hajji Musa drew the curtains in the room, lit the candle and placed the two glasses of water on either side of the candle. He took incense out of his pocket, put it in an ashtray and lit it.

When husband and wife returned with the children they were awed. There was an atmosphere of strangeness, of mystery, in the room. Hajji Musa looked solemn. He took the candle, held it about face level and said:

'Look, there is a halo around the flame.'

They looked and saw a faint halo.

He placed the candle on the table, took the glasses of water, held them above the flame and recited a verse from the Koran. When he had done he gave one glass to the boy and one to the girl.

'Drink, my children,' he said. They hesitated for a moment, but Bibi Fatima commanded them to drink the water.

'They will be well,' he said authoritatively. 'They can now go and play.'

He extinguished the candle, drew the curtains, and sat down on the settee. And he laughed, a full-throated, uproarious, felicitous laugh.

'Don't worry about the children. Allah has performed miracles and what are coughs and loss of appetites.' And he laughed again.

Bibi Fatima went to the kitchen to make tea and Jogee and I kept him company. She returned shortly with tea and cake.

'Jogee,' she said, 'I think Hajji Musa is greater than Dr Kamal. You remember last year Dr Kamal gave me medicines and ointments for my aching back and nothing came of it?'

'Hajji Musa is not an ordinary doctor.'

'What are doctors of today,' Hajji Musa said, biting into a large slice of cake, 'but chancers and frauds? What knowledge have they of religion and the spiritual mysteries?'

'Since when have you this power to heal, Hajji Musa?'

'Who can tell the ways of Allah, Bibi Fatima. Sometimes his gifts are given when we are born and sometimes when we are much older.'

'More tea?'

She filled the cup. He took another slice of cake.

'Last month I went to Durban and there was this woman, Jasuben, whom the doctors had declared insane. Even her own yogis and swamis had given her up. I took this woman in hand and today she is as sane as anyone else.'

'Hajji Musa, you know my back still gives me trouble. Dr Kamal's medicine gave me no relief. I have even stopped making roti and Jogee is very fond of roti.'

'You should let me examine your back some day,' the healer said, finishing his tea.

'Why not now?'

'Not today,' he answered protestingly. 'I have some business to attend to.'

'But Hajji Musa, it will only take a minute or two.'

'Well that's true, that's true.'

'Will you need the candle and water?'

'Yes.'

She hurriedly went to refill the glass with water.

'Please, Jogee and Ahmed, go into the kitchen for a while,' she said, returning.

We left the room, Jogee rather reluctantly. She shut the door. I sat down on a chair and looked at a magazine lying on the table. Jogee told me he was going to buy cigarettes and left. He was feeling nervous.

I was sitting close to the door and could hear Hajji Musa's voice and the rustle of clothing as he went on with the examination.

'I think it best if you lie down on the settee so that I can make a thorough examination ... Yes, that is better ... Is the pain here ... ? Bibi Fatima, you know the pain often has its origin lower down, in the lumbar region. Could you ease your ijar a little ... ? The seat of the pain is often here Don't be afraid.'

'I can feel it getting better already, Hajji Musa.'

'That is good. You are responding very well.'

There was silence for some time. When Jogee returned Hajji Musa was reciting a prayer in Arabic. Jogee puffed at his cigarette.

When Bibi Fatima opened the door she was smiling and looked flushed.

'Your wife will be well in a few days,' Hajji Musa assured the anxious man. 'And you will have your daily roti again. Now I must go.'

'Hajji Musa, but we must give you something for your trouble.'

'No nothing, Bibi Fatima. I forbid you.'

She was insistent. She told Jogee in pantomime (she showed him five fingers) how much money he should give. Jogee produced the money from his pocket, though inwardly protesting at his wife's willingness to pay a man who asked no fees. Bibi Fatima put the money into Hajji Musa's pocket.

In appearance Hajji Musa was a fat, pot-bellied, short, dark man, with glossy black wavy hair combed backwards with fastidious care. His face was always clean shaven. For some reason he never shaved in the bathroom, and every morning one saw him in the yard, in vest and pyjama trousers, arranging (rather precariously) his mirror and shaving equipment on the window-sill outside the kitchen and going through the ritual of cleaning his face with the precision of a surgeon. His great passion was talking and while shaving he would be conducting conversations with various people in the yard: with the hawker packing his fruit and vegetables in the cart; with the two wives of the motor mechanic Soni; with the servants coming to work.

Hajji Musa was a well-known man. At various times he had been a commercial traveller, insurance salesman, taxi driver, companion to dignitaries from India and Pakistan, Islamic missionary, teacher at a seminary, shopkeeper, matchmaker and hawker of ladies' underwear.

His career as a go-between in marriage transactions was a brief inglorious one that almost ended his life. One night there was fierce knocking at his door. As soon as he opened it an angry voice exploded: 'You liar! You come and tell me of dat good-for-nutting Dendar boy, dat he good, dat he ejucated, dat he good prospect. My foot and boot he ejucated! He sleep most time wit bitches, he drink and beat my daughter. When you go Haj? You nutting but liar. You baster! You baster!' And suddenly two shots from a gun rang out in quick succession. The whole incident took place so quickly that no one had any time to look at the man as he ran through the yard and escaped. When people reached Hajji Musa's door they found him prostrate, breathing hard and wondering why he was still alive (the bullets had passed between his legs). His wife and eight children were in a state of shock. They were revived with sugared water.

Hajji Musa's life never followed an even course: on some days one saw him riding importantly in the chauffeur-driven Mercedes of some wealthy merchant in need of his services; on others, one saw him in the yard, pacing meditatively from one end to the other, reciting verses from the Koran. Sometimes he would visit a friend, tell an amusing anecdote, laugh, and suddenly ask: 'Can you give me a few rands till tomorrow?' The friend would give him the money without expecting anything of tomorrow, for it was well-known that Hajji Musa, liberal with his own money, never bothered to return anyone else's.

Hajji Musa considered himself a specialist in the exorcism of evil jinn. He deprecated modern terms such as neurosis, schizophrenia, psychosis. 'What do doctors know about the power of satanic jinn? Only God can save people who are no longer themselves. I have proved this time and again. You don't believe me? Then come on Sunday night to my house and you will see.'

On Sunday night we were clustered around Hajji Musa in the yard. As his patient had not yet arrived, he regaled us with her history.

'She is sixteen. She is the daughter of Mia Mohammed the Market Street merchant. She married her cousin a few years ago. But things went wrong. Her mother-in-law disliked her. For months she has been carted from doctor to doctor, and from one psychiatrist to another, those fools. Tonight you will see me bring about a permanent cure.'

After a while a car drove into the yard, followed by two others. Several men – two of them tall, bearded brothers – emerged from the car, approached Hajji Musa and shook hands with him. They pointed to the second car.

'She is in that car, Hajji Musa.'

'Good, bring her into the house.' And he went inside.

There were several women in the second car. All alighted, but one who refused to come out. She shook her face and hands and cried, 'No! No! Don't take me in there, please! By Allah I am a good girl.'

The two brothers and several women stood beside the opened doors of the car and coaxed the young lady to come out.

'Sister, come, we are only visiting.'

'No, no, they are going to hit me.'

'No one is going to hit you,' one of the women said, getting into the car and sitting beside her. 'They only want to see you.'

'They can see me in the car. I am so pretty.'

Everyone living in the yard was present to witness the spectacle, and several children had clambered onto the bonnet of the car and were shouting: There she is! There she is! She is mad! She is mad!'

'Come now, Jamilla, come. The people are laughing at you,' one of the brothers said sternly.

Hajji Musa now appeared wearing a black cloak emblazoned with sequin-studded crescent moons and stars, and inscribed with Cufic writing in white silk. His sandals were red and his trousers white. His turban was of green satin and it had a large round ruby (artificial) pinned to it above his forehead.

He proceeded towards the car, looked at Jamilla, and then said to the bearded brothers, 'I will take care of her.' He put his head into the interior of the car, Jamilla recoiled in terror. The lady next to her held her and said, 'Don't be frightened. Hajji Musa intends no harm.'

'Listen, sister, come into the house. I have been expecting you.'

'No! No! I want to go home,' Jamilla began to cry.

'I won't let anyone hurt you.'

Hajji Musa tried to grab her hand, but she pushed herself backwards against the woman next to her, and screamed so loudly that for a moment the healer seemed to lose his nerve. He turned to the brothers.

'The evil jinn is in her. Whatever I do now, please forgive me.'

He put his foot into the interior of the car, gripped one arm of the terrified Jamilla and smacked her twice with vehemence.

'Come out jinn! Come out jinn!' he shouted and dragged her towards the door of the car. The woman beside Jamilla pushed her and punched her on her back.

'Please help,' Hajji Musa said, and the two brothers pulled the screaming Jamilla out of the car.

'Drive the jinn into the house!' And they punched and pushed Jamilla towards the house. She pleaded with several spectators for help and then in desperation clung to them. But they shook her off and one or two even took the liberty of punching her and pulling her hair.

Jamilla was pushed into the house and the door closed on her and several of the privileged who were permitted to witness the exorcism ceremony. As soon as she passed through a narrow passage and entered a room she quietened.

The room was brilliantly lit and a fire was burning in the grate. A red carpet stretched from wall to wall and on the window-sill incense was burning in brass bowls. In front of the grate were two brass plates containing sun-dried red chillies.

We removed our shoes and sat down on the carpet. Jamilla was made to sit in front of the grate. She was awed and looked about at the room and the people. Several women seated themselves near her. Hajji Musa then began to recite the chapter 'The Jinn' from the Koran. We sat with bowed heads. When he had done he moved towards the grate. His wife came into the room with a steel tray and a pair of tongs. Hajji Musa took some burning pieces of coal and heaped them on the tray. Then he scattered the red chillies over the coals. Smoke rose from the tray and filled the room with an acrid suffocating smell. He seated himself beside Jamilla and asked the two brothers to sit near her as well. He pressed Jamilla's head over the tray and at the same time recited a verse from the Koran in a loud voice. Jamilla choked, seemed to scream mutely and tried to lift her head, but Hajji Musa held her.

As the smell of burning chillies was unbearable, some of us went outside for a breath of fresh air. Aziz Khan said to us:

'That primitive ape is prostituting our religion with his hocus-pocus. He should be arrested for assault.'

We heard Jamilla screaming and we returned quickly to the room. We saw Hajji Musa and the two brothers beating her with their sandals and holding her face over the coals.

'Out Iblis! Out Jinn!' Hajji Musa shouted and belaboured her.

At last Jamilla fell into a swoon.

'Hold her, Ismail and Hafiz.' Hajji Musa sprinkled her face with water and read a prayer. Then he asked the two brothers to pick her up and take her into an adjoining room. They laid her on a bed.

'When she wakes up the jinn will be gone,' Hajji Musa predicted confidently.

We went outside for a while. Aziz Khan asked a few of us to go with him in his car to the police station. But on the way he surprised us by changing his mind.

'It's not our business,' he said, and drove back to the yard.

When we returned Jamilla had opened her eyes and was sobbing quietly.

'Anyone can ask Jamilla if she remembers what happened to her.'

Someone asked her and she shook her head.

'See,' said the victorious man, 'it was the evil jinn that was thrashed out of her body. He is gone!'

There had been the singing of hymns, chanting and the jingling of bells since the late afternoon, and as evening approached there was great excitement in the yard. Everyone knew of the great event that was to take place that evening: the Hindu fire-walker was going to give a demonstration.

'There is nothing wonderful about walking on fire,' Hajji Musa declared in a scornful tone. 'The Hindus think they are performing miracles. Bah! Miracles!' And he exploded in laughter. 'What miracles can their many gods perform, I ask you? Let them extract a jinn or heal the sick and then talk of miracles.'

'But can you walk on fire or only cook on fire?' Dolly asked sardonically. There was laughter and merriment.

'Both, my dear man, both. Anyone who cooks on fire can walk on fire.'

'If anyone can let him try,' said the law student Soma. 'In law words are not enough; evidence has to be produced.'

'Funny you lawyers never get done with words. After gossiping for days you ask for a postponement.'

Everyone laughed boisterously.

'Hajji Musa,' Dolly tried again, 'can you walk on fire?'

'Are you joking, Dolly? When I can remove a jinn, what is walking on fire? Have you seen a jinn?'

'No.'

'See one and then talk. Evil jinn live in hell. What is walking on fire to holding one of hell's masters in your hands?'

'I say let him walk on fire and then talk of jinn,' said Rama the dwarfish Hindu watchmaker, but he walked away fearing to confront Hajji Musa.

'That stupid Hindu thinks I waste my time in performing tricks. I am not a magician.'

A fire was now lit in the yard. Wood had been scattered over an area of about twenty feet by six feet. An attendant was shovelling coal and another using the rake to spread it evenly.

Meanwhile, in a room in the yard, the voices of the chanters were rising and the bells were beginning to jingle madly. Every now and then a deeper, more resonant chime would ring out, and a voice would lead the chanters to a higher pitch. In the midst of the chanters, facing a small altar on which were placed a tiny earthenware bowl containing a burning wick, a picture of the god Shiva surrounded by votive offerings of marigold flowers, rice and coconut, sat the fire-walker in a cross-legged posture.

The yard was crowded. Chairs were provided but these were soon occupied. The balconies were packed and several agile children climbed onto rooftops and seated themselves on the creaking zinc. A few dignitaries were also present.

The chanters emerged from the doorway. In their midst was the fire-walker, his eyes focused on the ground. He was like a man eroded of his own will, captured by the band of chanters. They walked towards the fire which was now a glowing bed, with blue flames leaping here and there.

The chanters grouped themselves near the fire and went on with their singing and bell-ringing, shouting refrains energetically. Then, as though life had suddenly flowed into him, the fire-walker detached himself from the group and went towards the fire. It was a tense moment. The chanters were gripped by frenzy. The coal bed glowed. He placed his right foot on the fire gently, tentatively, as though measuring its intensity, and then walked swiftly over from end to end. He was applauded. Two boys now offered him coconuts in trays. He selected two, and then walked over the inferno again, rather slowly this time, and as he walked he banged the coconuts against his head several times until they cracked and one saw the snowy insides. His movement now became more like a dance than a walk, as though his feet gloried in their triumph over the fire. The boys offered him more coconuts and he went on breaking them against his head.

While the fire-walker was demonstrating his salamander-like powers, an argument developed between Aziz Khan and Hajji Musa.

'He is not walking over the fire,' Hajji Musa said. 'Our eyes are being deceived.'

'Maybe your eyes are being deceived, but not mine,' Aziz answered.

'If you know anything about yogis then you will know how they can pass off the unreal for the real.'

'What do you mean by saying if I know anything about yogis?'

'He thinks he knows about everything under the sun,' Hajji Musa said jeeringly to a friend. He turned to Aziz.

'Have you been to India to see the fakirs and yogis?'

'No, and I don't intend to.'

'Well, I have been to India and know more than you do.'

'I have not been to India, but what I do know is that you are a fraud.'

'Fraud! Huh!'

'Charlatan! Humbug!'

'I say, Aziz!' With a swift movement Hajji Musa clutched Aziz Khan's wrist.

'You are just a big-talker and one day I shall shut your mouth for you.'

'Fraud! Crook! You are a disgrace to Islam. You with your chillies and jinn!'

'Sister ... !' This remark Hajji Musa uttered in Gujarati.

'Why don't you walk over the fire? It's an unreal fire.' And Aziz laughed sardonically.

'Yes, let him walk,' said the watchmaker. 'Hajji Musa big-talker.'

'The fire is not as hot as any of your jinn, Hajji Musa,' Dolly said slyly, with an ironic chuckle.

'Dolly, anyone can walk on fire if he knows the trick.'

'I suppose you know,' Aziz said tauntingly.

'Of course I do.'

'Then why don't you walk over the fire?'

'Jinn are hotter!' Dolly exclaimed.

'Fraud! Hypocrite! Degraded infidel, you will never walk. I dare you!'

'I will show you, you fool. I will show you what I can do.'

'What can you show but your lying tongue, and beat up little girls!'

'You sister ... ! I will walk.'

While the argument had been raging, many people had gathered around them and ceased to look at the Hindu fire-walker. Now, when Hajji Musa accepted the challenge, he was applauded.

Hajji Musa removed his shoes and socks and rolled up his trousers. All eyes in the yard were now focused on him. Some shouted words of encouragement and others clapped their hands. Mr Darsot, though, tried to dissuade him.

'Hajji Musa, I don't think you should attempt walking on fire.'

But Dolly shouted in his raucous voice:
'Hajji Musa, show them what you are made of!'

Hajji Musa, determined and intrepid, went towards the fire. The Hindu fire-walker was now resting for a while, his body and clothes wet with sweat and juice from broken coconuts, and the chanters' voices were low. When Hajji Musa reached the fire he faltered. His body tensed with fear. Cautiously he lifted his right foot over the glowing mass. But any thought he might have had of retreat, of giving up Aziz Khan's challenge and declaring himself defeated, was dispelled by the applause he received.

Crying out in a voice that was an invocation to God to save him, he stepped on the inferno:

'Allah is great!'

What happened to Hajji Musa was spoken of long afterwards. Badly burnt, he was dragged out of the fire, drenched with water and smothered with rags, and taken to hospital.

We went to visit him. We expected to find a man humiliated, broken. We found him sitting up in bed, swathed in bandages, but as ebullient and resilient as always, with a bevy of young nurses eagerly attending to him.

'Boys, I must say fire-walking is not for me. Showmanship ... that's for magicians and crowd-pleasers ... those seeking cheap publicity.'

And he laughed in his usual way until the hospital corridors resounded.

The Target

Mahmood was the target of many fists. One would see him running down Terrace Road, a crowd of pursuers at his heels. They would catch him, contract their biceps and treat him as a punching-ball until the people in the yard where he lived ran to his rescue.

Mahmood was my relative and I would often visit his mother and sister. He was ruddy in complexion, fat, with a brilliantined wad of brownish hair on his small head and dark grey eyes beneath sleek eyebrows.

There was a time when Mahmood was involved in a protracted war (largely waged by the opposite party) with the Kanti family. He decided to propose marriage to Safia, a thirteen year old school girl, but he went to her house on his own instead of sending an emissary as was the custom. On the first occasion he was chased out of the house by the girl's mother and sisters wielding broomsticks and kitchen utensils. On the second occasion Safia's father and brothers displayed their pugilistic skill. Mahmood persisted in his pursuit of the youthful Safia despite the continual beatings by her family. They would either besiege him in the street and use him as a volleyball, or allow him to enter the house and use him as a guinea-pig in a variety of experiments in martyrdom. But Mahmood miraculously not only survived but won the admiration of Safia who pleaded with her parents to end hostilities. This earned her the anger of her family and she was banished to her uncle's home in a distant country town. But she communicated secretly with Mahmood from there. Her hero reached her and took her away. The fugitives were found within an hour, at the railway station waiting for a train. Mahmood was basted and bundled into the train when it arrived and Safia taken captive. When Safia's parents came to hear of the incident they immediately sent for her. They were convinced she was deflowered – anything could have happened to her during the hour she was with Mahmood – and decided to go to Mahmood's house and offer her hand in marriage. He promptly rejected the offer ('I have my dignity,' he explained later) and suffered another tempest of blows.

Thereafter Mahmood found it hazardous to walk in Mint Road. 'The road is not theirs,' he declared truculently. Whenever he did he was sure to find a stone hurled at him, or a woman's voice rich in curses, or Safia's brothers sprinting at his heels as he fled.

One day a gang of whites came chasing Mahmood into the yard. He screamed for help. Fortunately for him Solomon and Dolly were present. They cornered the gang and made good use of the opportunity, which did not come often, to beat up some whites.

After a few days we were surprised to see a tribal warrior fully accoutred, with horns on his head, guarding the door of Mahmood's house. His wife was also present, a stout woman lavishly bedecked with beads from head to foot. When I asked Mahmood why he had engaged the couple he answered cryptically:

'I am practising integration.'

The warrior with his shield, spear and club became the object of a great deal of curiosity. Children were always staring at him and people took photographs. He would pose for the photographers, and when they had done he would go up to them, stretch out his left hand and raise his spear with his right hand. Money would quickly be put into his palm. The only word in his English vocabulary was 'Good!' which he uttered with a zestful bellow. His wife assisted Mahmood's mother with the household chores, and when she was not busy would sit beside her husband in the sun, combing her pyramid of hair and applying lipstick to her lips and cheeks and looking into a tiny piece of broken mirror.

With the warrior for protection Mahmood strutted about without fear of attack. Soon he began going out with the warrior at night.

'Where do you go with him?' I asked.

'Visiting friends,' he answered. But one day I discovered that he was visiting enemies rather than friends when I saw the warrior's club stained with blood.

Mahmood's period of respite from the fists of his enemies did not last long. Somebody reported to the police that he was employing the warrior and his wife without the necessary permit. The couple were arrested, charged, fined (Mahmood paid the fines) and ordered to remove themselves to their tribal reserve. Mahmood was fined as well for 'employing unregistered labour'.

Shortly after the warrior left, Mahmood became one of the 'directors' of the Blue Danube Social Club in Mayfair, as a consequence of which occupation he on several occasions returned home with a blackened eye, a sprained wrist or a bruised head. After one particularly bad spell of directing he told me:

'There was a whole span of ducktails at the Club. My father always told me not to interfere with ducktails. But they got stuck into me.'

In Mahmood's thoughts his late father was an ever-present reality whose precepts he faithfully upheld, though his actions were seldom in accord with them and often antithetical.

'But why don't you resign as a director?'

'I have a stake in the Club.'

'But you will never get out of trouble.'

'They will get tired of beating me. They will come to know me better and they will stop. My father always said that if people know you, you will never get into trouble.'

It was an unusual way of getting known. Mahmood did not seem to realize that as there were many fists in need of a target it would take an inordinately long time before everyone came to know him.

One day Mahmood introduced me to 'Najma'. She was a white. She was a short girl, gawky in her walk, exposing much of her fleshy legs. Her face was a fashion photographer's dream: a chubby pink face, a mob of blond hair, cerulean eyes in a penumbra of cobalt eye shadow, cheeks rouged and lips vermilion. I did not inquire where he had met her but I inferred from her appearance that she was a frequenter of his Club.

'She is going to change her religion,' Mahmood said. 'She is joining us.'

I looked at 'Najma'. She smiled approvingly.

'Aziz Khan is giving her religious lessons.'

'A good idea.'

Mahmood came closer to me and whispered:

'The gang is against her changing religion.'

'Gang?'

'Those who come with her to the Club.'

I saw 'Najma' often in Mahmood's house. Aziz Khan's religious instructions were taking effect. She was now of little interest to a photographer. She no longer used make-up, and wore a black scarf that covered her head, her forehead and her shoulders. Her pants were pantaloon-type and her dress a wide smock. She was sitting on the edge of the settee, swinging her legs.

'How do you like your new religion?' I asked her.

'I am getting used to it. My instructor says I am making good progress. It will all be very easy, he tells me, because Christians were Muslims before the priests came to spoil everything.'

As I was not aware of this historical fact I did not comment.

'My instructor tells me that I must be at all times "soberly and modestly clad" and I am doing my best as you can see. Is that not so Mahmood?'

Mahmood agreed.

'Sometimes he is so amusing. He tells me that doing, you know what, is a blessing and compulsory.'

She tittered.

'And I must not talk to foreign males. But that is a little difficult as you can see.'

She tittered again.

'I shouldn't be talking to you because you may … '

'That's au-right,' Mahmood interrupted. 'He is one of us. Come, let's have lunch.'

Mahmood's mother and sister had laid the table and had retired to an inner room. They were not very enthusiastic about 'Najma' and pretended she was not present.

Mahmood filled 'Najma's' plate with food and spoonfuls of pepper relish. 'Najma' valiantly swallowed the food and relish. She drank glasses of water.

'She must get used to our food,' Mahmood said, looking at her. 'Inside and out she must be a Muslim.' He spooned more relish for her.

'My father always said that if you convert someone you must do it properly.'

When I left, Mahmood and 'Najma' were sitting together on the settee, holding hands.

A week later I asked Mahmood how 'Najma' was getting on with her religious instructions. He answered:

'That guy is wasting her time.'

From the scornful tone of his voice I gathered that Aziz Khan was not confining himself strictly to religious prescriptions.

A month later a few friends and I were in Mayfair at night and decided to visit the Blue Danube Club. The Club was on the second floor of the building, above a warehouse. The doorkeeper, a testy youth, would not let us in without payment and we asked to see Mahmood. Grudgingly he went to fetch Mahmood and when he came Mahmood persuaded the youth to let us in by explaining that we were visitors from Durban. We climbed the stairs and entered a large room lit by coloured lights. A band was playing in a corner and couples were dancing, I saw 'Najma' (she was no longer 'soberly and modestly clad') tightly clasped in the arms of a youth. I pointed her out to Mahmood.

'She is jolling again with guys,' he said.

We watched the dancers as they began to jive to rousing music.

'If any of you feel for a dance go ahead,' Mahmood said to us.

We declined and said we preferred to watch.

After a while 'Najma' spotted me and coming over with her partner said 'Hi! Enjoying yourself?' and left the Club with her partner. I saw Mahmood scowling at her as she went out.

The next day I heard that Mahmood had been so severely beaten that he required treatment in hospital. I went to see him. He looked like a mummy. His head was bandaged; his one eye swollen and closed; his one arm in plaster.

'What happened?' I asked.

'The gang got me.'

He lifted his head with an agonized groan.

'My father always told me to keep away from white girls – and clubs.'

Aziz Khan

I FIRST MET AZIZ KHAN – described in various Muslim journals as the 'author of the renowned pamphlets *Muslims in Decay* and the *Decline and Fall of the Morality of Muslims*' and as the 'illustrious modern Saracen' – the day he handed me a cyclostyled copy of his pamphlet *The Degeneracy of Muslim Marriages* at a wedding reception.

When I entered the hall decorated with balloons and tinsel, the tables heaped with cake and delicacies, I saw a number of his pamphlets lying on the floor and being trampled upon by the guests. The hall had been divided into two sections, one for the gaily dressed womenfolk, one for the men.

As the bride and bridegroom had not yet arrived I decided to read Aziz Khan's pamphlet. It began:

> 'One is amazed and aghast at the complete and utter degeneracy of our present-day Muslim marriages. The pristine purity of our hallowed ceremonies and customs has been sullied by the importation of Westernized forms dating back atavistically to the days when naked European heathens sojourned in primeval forests. It is about time that someone brought the shocking state of affairs to the notice of the public. One has only to look at the womenfolk to understand the extent to which the mania for modernism has advanced. Our women are no longer soberly and modestly clad at wedding functions, but shamelessly manifest themselves in shining gaudy frippery, displaying their bosoms and buttocks in the most outrageous manner to leering, lustful, lascivious eyes. Is there anything more odious than the sari – essentially a Hindu garment?'

I looked at the women in the hall. They were beautifully dressed. Several girls in pink dresses, glossy hair piled on their heads, eyes glamorously blackened with kohl and the palms of their hands dyed with henna, were moving from table to table arranging flowers in vases. I looked at the men grouped around tables, chatting to one another in a self-contained way. I read on:

> 'The most despicable of all practices frowned upon by our Holy Prophet is the mingling of sexes in halls where wedding functions are

held. During our so-called Islamic weddings all kinds of shameless fraternisation between the sexes occur, spiced with lascivious talk that would shame the very sons of Iblis. Have we Muslims degenerated to such an extent that we are unable to see the morass of sin we are wallowing in and the slippery spirals leading us to the fire of Doom? Where are our Ulamas and Molvis, the learned men steeped in Islamic law and traditions? They too seem to have succumbed to the modernistic fad of the intermingling of the sexes.'

There was the loud hooting of cars outside the hall. This signalled the arrival of the bride. She soon entered with her train and walked along the aisle that separated the sexes. She was dressed in the usual white, The bridesmaids were dressed in blue. They went towards the stage, climbed several steps and seated themselves.

As the bridegroom and his party had not yet arrived I read on:
'As for that ritual which Muslims have imbibed from the dehumanized Westerners, I refer to that pagan institution the Betrothal, the less said about it the better. Totally foreign to the pristine purity of Muslim culture, one can only scoff at the despicable practice of giving an engagement ring (the man actually holds the woman's hand to fit the ring on the finger) and very often indulging in that impure act, a legacy of filthy barbarians – kissing!'

Then there followed a paragraph on the 'endless expenses involved in these so-called civilized weddings'; another on the 'diabolical desire to have better and bigger weddings', and another on 'the waste of food that could feed battalions of starving people for months'. The final paragraph read:
'And as for that practice of displaying the bride on the stage so that everyone can leer at her and imagine all sorts of lewd things, such as what is going to happen to her on her bridal couch and so forth – the practice is so heinous and satanic that I can hardly bring myself to refer to it. All decent people will be revolted at this anti-Islamic, pro-Occidental custom of exposing the bride ... '

The bridegroom and his party entered the hall. The bridegroom went towards the stage and after shaking his bride's hand joined his friends at a table.

As I folded the pamphlet the very man who had handed it to me at the door settled down in a vacant seat opposite and smilingly said:

'Have you found my treatise interesting?'

'Very.'

'I thank you,' he said, extending a hand to me.

He did not consider it odd in any way to be present at a wedding reception (I presumed he had been invited) after issuing a pamphlet of strictures. He seemed to be enjoying himself and I did not care to question his presence.

This same Aziz Khan not long after ignited one of the greatest religious issues among Muslims, that concerning the beard of man.

It was on a Friday when people went as usual to the Newtown mosque for prayers, which were conducted by Molvi Haroon. Afterwards the same dignitary delivered a lecture which consisted of a medley of aphorisms, historical anecdotes, Sufism and moral precepts on the keeping of beards. The beard, the Molvi declared, was the mark of a Muslim and the beardless ones should not scoff at those who were devout enough to cultivate beards.

The reference to the beard was not a matter for controversy – the congregation regarded the lecture as a verbal exercise and would have gone on merrily using the razor. But Aziz Khan immediately rose from the carpet and challenged the Molvi.

'Molvi Haroon, can you quote the passage in the Holy Koran which unequivocally states that the beard is compulsory on all Muslims?'

Issuing a challenge in the mosque is unusual. Everyone was jolted. Molvi Haroon smiled pityingly at his adversary and shrewdly posed the following question:

'Tell me, did the messenger of Allah, our holy Prophet, have a beard or not?'

Aziz asked his question again, and again the Molvi posed his parrying question. It was a stalemate. Infuriated, Aziz walked out of the mosque, followed by some twenty of his disciples.

After a few days Aziz Khan's pamphlet on the beard made its appearance. Part of it read:

> 'The men who claim to be the repositories of Islamic wisdom, the Molvis and other self-styled pundits, have again and again exposed themselves to the public as a set of fools. What could be more asinine and moronic than the statement by that doyen of priests, Molvi Haroon, that those without beards are not Muslims? What knowledge has this rebarbative microbe of the ineluctable beauty of Islam ... '

Aziz Khan's pamphlet made the issue a public one, and the Islamic Academy hurriedly convened a Muslim Council to settle the matter. Aziz Khan's fame reached its zenith. Everyone marvelled at his audacity in challenging an army of luminaries. He went about in the company of his disciples, addressing meetings, some of which ended in violence between the bearded and the beardless, with victory usually going to the beardless as they were in the majority.

After a week-end of deliberation the Muslim Council issued a counter-pamphlet. It began:

> 'Proudly they strut about our streets, with naked chins shamelessly exposed, professing themselves to be reformers and doctors of learning. But any foolish ape can see that they are driven by their base egos to bark like mad dogs, casting aspersions on the beard of our Prophet (on whom be peace).'

The pamphlet went on to describe the historical circumstances that led to Muslims cultivating beards: their opposition to the *Mushrikeen* (heathens), the *Cafirs* (unbelievers), and hatred of the fire-worshipping Persians. It continued:

> 'The beard has been the pillar of Islam from the beginning when Allah drove his beloved Adam from paradise to the present day when the world is infested with beardless Cafirs. Who can deny that Adam – the handsomest man in the annals of Creation – possessed a beard? We ask these hypocritical reformers this simple question: Did Adam have a razor and blades? Who but the valiant sons of Islam sporting their beards smashed that mighty of mighties, the Roman Empire? And who but the bearded warriors of Islam withstood the avalanche of pig-eating crusaders? But, alas! when the beards of the

Muslims came under the razors of the infidels their glorious empires vanished along with them.'

The final paragraph stated:

'We take this opportunity to issue this dire warning to the beardless mob of Islam-haters, that if you continue maligning the beard of our Prophet, the Almighty will send ambassadors to BREAK YOUR NECKS. May the curse of Allah and his *Malla-ika* (angels) and of the *Ambiya* (contemporaries of the Prophet) and the entire *Ummate Muslima* (Muslim world) fall upon you.'

To this pamphlet Aziz Khan replied with another, concluding with these words: 'If the so-called Muslim Council thinks that there are any other ambassadors of Allah than the Prophets of Islam, then on the Day of Reckoning they will be consigned to roast on the spits of Hell.'

A few months later Aziz Khan, who was a commercial traveller, was forced to stop his car along a country road by another car that blocked the way. Three men emerged. Aziz recognized Gool and his associates.

'Follow that car,' Gool said, opening the door of Aziz's ear and getting in. The two men returned to Gool's car and started it.

'I have some business with you,' Gool said in explanation, lighting a cigar.

'Where are you taking me?' Aziz asked.

'You will see.'

'I was on my way to Paruk's shop. He is expecting me.'

'He can wait.'

The car ahead was travelling at speed and Aziz was lagging behind.

'Drive faster.'

'The dust,' Aziz protested.

'Shall I take over the wheel?'

Aziz pressed the accelerator. The dust from the two cars swirled in the air.

'The dust.'

'Keep up.'

'I can't see.'

'Keep up.'

Aziz quailed. He was driving at a dangerous speed along a rutted road behind a car spewing dust.

Suddenly the realization came to him that Gool and his associates were the 'ambassadors'.

'You are the ambassador?' Aziz asked.

'What?' Gool said in a tone of such menace that Aziz froze.

'Slow down,' Gool said. And as if the driver of the car ahead had been commanded together with Aziz Khan, the two cars slackened speed and came to a stop beside a clump of trees.

'Get out.'

'What are you going to do to me?'

'You will see.'

'Listen, Muslim brother, look at yourself. You are without a beard.'

'Beard? I am handsome enough without one.'

'But ... '

'Stop fooling. Get out!'

Aziz got out of the car while Gool remained seated. Gool's associates emerged from their car and came towards him.

'Muslim brothers, you are without beards!' Aziz shouted and began to run. 'Muslim brothers you are without ... '

Gladiators

Mr Rijhumal Rajespery, the principal of the Tagore Indian High School, lived on the first floor of a two-storeyed building. He was a bachelor. His state of bachelorhood was not the result of his insensitivity to feminine allure, but of his positive dislike of all things Indian. He considered Indians to be the 'filthiest and most uncouth denizens on the earth's crust'. Once when Ebrahim spoke of marriage to him, he answered:

'Are you suggesting that I terminate my single state of man by marrying an Indian Yahoo? The day I marry, I shall marry a white woman.'

'Are you ashamed of being an Indian, Mr Rajespery?'

'For your information I am not a common Indian. I am a pure Dravidian.'

Cleanliness was his forte and his obsession. His suite of rooms – a polished brass plate outside the door blazed: Mr R.A.J. Rajespery B.A. – was carpeted and expensively furnished. His clothing was immaculate. His middle-aged body, consisting mainly of bones, was at all times spruce and smelling of perfume and aftershave lotion. His sparse gently-waving hair was glued to his head; his moustache was the barber's masterpiece. His motor-car, a black Citroën ('a car in advance of its time') was polished to a mirror's gloss by his white-clad servant Anna.

Though Mr Rajespery's manners were impeccable, he derided our frailties and foibles in sadistic street sermons. 'The words "Thank you", "Please", "Pardon me" do not appear in the vocabulary of Indians. You are a mob of unruly Yahoos. I find your manners odious and crude.' And he would walk hurriedly away towards his car, open the door, operate the pneumatic suspension so that his car rose from its low-slung position, and drive away with a look of utter disdain.

At school Mr Rajespery spent his time in dealing with 'long-haired, unproductive louts'. He fought an endless battle to have recalcitrant pupils march in military fashion, show eternal respect for superiors, obey instructions and 'behave like Europeans'. He earned many uncomplimentary nicknames, but eventually the word Yahoo recoiled in vengeance upon him and became permanently his. It was a name that must have flayed him, for schoolboys 'Yahooed' from stairs, balconies, corridors and dark recesses and the name reverberated through the streets like some wild call in jungle terrain.

Mr Rajespery was a 'dedicated student of the Fine Arts'. His artistic pretensions were displayed in canvasses in which a vibrant orange-red dominated his paintings of landscapes – his only subject – where the oil ran in surrealist rivers of fire and destroyed perspective. On occasions he would exhibit his paintings on the balcony. Once he constructed a number of miniature homes, as architects do, with wood, plaster, paper and other materials, and opened the exhibition to the public. In explanation he said: 'I have been commissioned by the authorities to plan the new Indian residential suburb of Lenasia and these are models of some of the homes that will be erected.' We examined the models with interest. 'Please remember it is a solo effort, a solo effort. My only hope and prayer is that the Yahoos won't convert the suburb into a slum. I may also mention that I have been commissioned by my educational superiors to draw up the new syllabus for Fine Arts in schools. Indian children are generally ignorant about art, not to mention a certain primary school principal.'

The primary school principal was Mr Rajah who lived on the ground floor of the same building. He was a fat satyr of a man, a lover of the flesh of goats and the flesh of fat women, On several occasions I carried messages from him to certain well-nourished women in Fordsburg. He had five children from his fat wife Halima. He was an extremely affable man and was always ready to take us for a drive in his red Chevrolet ornamented with chrome-plated accessories to various cafés and fruit shops and regale us with confectionery, fruit and cool drinks, 'Help yourselves, boys, it's on me,' he would say, with the owner looking wide-eyed and pretending to be pleased. We later discovered that the various fruit shops and cafés belonged to parents of children who attended his school and that 'It's on me' hardly meant at his expense. His kitchen was well-stocked with provisions, from spiced ox-tongue to trays of choice fruit, and the provisions seemed to increase in quantity when end-of-year examination results at his school were about to be released.

Mr Rajespery and Mr Rajah were enemies. The origin of their antagonism lay in their differing temperaments rather than in any quarrel over something specific. One day we were clustered around Mr Rajah who was sitting on a chair outside his doorstep. He was talking to us about Mr Rajespery.

'He thinks he is superior because he lives upstairs and has carpets in his rooms. And all those whites visiting him? A lot of stupid school inspectors. Yesterday I heard him telling Mr Marks that if I so much as looked at his paintings he would have me arrested for it would be "tantamount to theft". Those were his words. His paintings are fit for the rubbish heap of an asylum.'

We laughed and just then we saw Mr Rajespery going up the stairs to his apartment in the company of a white man.

'Some people always attach themselves to their masters,' Mr Rajah said loudly.

We tittered satirically.

Mr Rajespery, smarting at the sarcasm, proceeded to his rooms. We remained with Mr Rajah for some time while he told us anecdotes and cracked jokes, most of them of an indecent kind.

Mr Rajespery and the man came down the stairs. We watched in silence. Good manners demanded that Mr Rajespery accompany his visitor to his car in the street. On his way back Mr Rajah addressed him:

'Stop Mr White!'

But Mr Rajespery quickly climbed several steps of the stairs and then stopped.

'Some people's manners are putrid.'

'Some people use Elizabeth Arden's complexion creams but there is no white result!'

We laughed derisively.

'If you speak to me address me properly, Mr Rajah.'

'You can only run after whites.'

'I am proud of that. They are civilized.'

Ebrahim decided to intervene in the argument.

'Mr Rajespery, the whites are oppressors.'

'I am afraid I don't understand you politicians. They are our superiors.'

'We Indians have a culture. What have your superiors?' Mr Rajah asked.

'Culture? If you call eating foul-smelling curry culture, eating betel leaf and spitting all over culture, living in filth culture. Has anyone in India ever invented such a thing as a bicycle, not to speak of an advanced machine like my Citroën? Indians are a lot of unproductive morons. Yahoos!'

And he walked up the stairs to his apartment in triumph.

Mr Rajah felt beaten.

'You boys should not take this lying down. He has insulted you. Don't worry about me. I'll get him someday.'

When the fight between the two eventually took place it was by proxy. Anna, slender and tall, represented Mr Rajespery; Elizabeth, fat and short, represented Mr Rajah. The battle had its origin in a squabble which started after a basin of dirty water had been emptied over Mr Rajespery's Citroën. Mr Rajespery came down the stairs, stopped halfway when he saw Mr Rajah, and accused him of having sullied his car. Mr Rajah retreated to the safety of his doorway.

'Why don't you instruct your servant to empty your filthy water somewhere else?'

'Why do you park your car on the pavement?'

'I will park it where I prefer.'

Mr Rajespery's servant stood beside him, dressed like a nurse, and Mr Rajah's servant beside him, dowdy and ugly.

'Anna, did you see that creature empty the dish water?'

'I saw her, master.'

'You didn't see me,' shouted Elizabeth.

'I did, with my own eyes,' answered Anna, placing her index-fingers on her eye-lids.

The two women now took up the argument in an African tongue. They spoke menacingly and shook their hands wildly. Suddenly Anna came down the stairs, Elizabeth proceeded towards her and they confronted each other.

They began with a sort of skirmish during which they tried to tear off each others' clothes. Anna's starched cap went flying, the straps of her apron were forced apart, and her blouse was ripped off. She in turn tugged at Elizabeth's dress; the cheap material offered no resistance.

Anna delivered several hard punches to Elizabeth's body. Elizabeth clasped her and the two women fell and rolled along the pavement. They threshed, wrestled, pounded with clenched fists. When they were tired they rested for a while, their hands gripping each other's, their legs intertwined.

The battle had moved a short distance from where it began. Mr Rajespery was left standing on the stairs and Mr Rajah in his doorway.

The two clasped naked bodies were rolling on the pavement again. Suddenly Anna screamed: Elizabeth had her teeth embedded in her arm.

Several people threw themselves on the women and, at length, managed to free Anna's arm from Elizabeth's teeth. Anna lay on the pavement, her arm bleeding. We ran to Mr Rajespery who was still standing on the stairs to tell him of Anna's condition, and that he should take her to a doctor.

'To a doctor? I am a doctor,' he said, staring at us.

Mr Rajah stood at his door, his thumbs in his braces, and laughed triumphantly. Mr Rajespery, seeming oblivious of him, descended the stairs, went towards his car, opened the door, entered and operated the automatic suspension. The car rose to its. maximum height, then went down, rose again, went down again. Mr Rajah came to sit on the fender of the car, and laughed jeeringly as the car rose and sank. Suddenly Mr Rajespery darted out of the car in a swift menacing movement that shocked Mr

Rajah who fell and sprained his ankle, bounded over the steps of the stairs, entered his apartment and locked himself in.

Someone took Anna to a doctor. Fortunately her wound was not serious. But more serious was the state of her master's mind. Next morning he was seen sitting in his Citroën, speaking to himself, shaking his fists at those looking at him, and refusing to come out. Many people came to see him; children milled around his car; and everybody laughed at the sight of Mr Rajespery in his black Citroën, going up and down.

Black and White

SHIREEN WAS THE DAUGHTER OF THE WIDOW Wadia. She was pretty in a paganish way, with black eyes peering impishly through unruly hair. She wore her skirts daringly short and when she wore trousers they were always so tight that they displayed her well-formed thighs. She was a girl full of gaiety and wit, at times skittishly anarchic and irresponsible, and none of us with whom she engaged in love-making interludes ever came to believe she could be possessed permanently.

One day she said to us:

'Guess what, boys? I am in love.'

We laughed.

'All right then, someone is in love with me.'

We were eager to know.

'He will be here tonight. Keep a look-out for his motor-cycle.'

'Is he one of those cycle-obsessed morons?'

'You are all jealous. He has blond hair.'

'A white!'

'Yes, white like cheese!'

'Like cheese?'

'Any way, he smells it.'

We laughed.

We kept a look-out for Shireen's lover that night in Terrace Road. She came to join us on the pavement outside Hassen's Shoe Store, with mock impatience smoked several cigarettes and threw them half-smoked into the gutter.

'He will never come to Fordsburg at night,' I said.

'You think he is afraid of people like you?'

'Where did you meet him?'

'In Mayfair.'

'In Mayfair! A poor white!' Nizam exclaimed.

'Jealous? Of course I met him in Mayfair and what's wrong with that? A Mayfair white is as good as any other white. He's got a white skin, hasn't he? He says he digs me.'

Suddenly the roar of a motor-cycle resounded and we saw Shireen's lover approaching. Shireen ran towards him, waving her hands and shouting:

'Hi Harold! Hi Harold!'

We watched him slacken speed and steer his motor-cycle towards the street kerb. Shireen jumped on the motor-cycle's petrol tank and revved the accelerator in triumph and waved at us excitedly.

We went towards them. Shireen introduced us. Harold did not bother to get off his motor-cycle or shake our hands.

He came every Friday evening to meet Shireen. They would go into the doorway recess of Hassen's Shoe Store. Occasionally we watched them from the opposite pavement, and when the passing beam from a motor-car exposed them momentarily, we saw them embracing. He whispered to her incessantly. He was a lean eager-eyed youth, with a receding chin; he was always dressed in jeans and a leather lumber-jacket ornamented with emblems of motor-cars and motor-cycles. His motor-cycle was a powerful gleaming machine that seemed to compensate in some way for his lack of personality.

As time went on the novelty of having a white lover seemed to wear thin and Shireen began to taunt him. On one occasion she ran to us gathered on the opposite pavement and said:

'Guess what, boys? He wants me to go with him to the mine dumps.'

'Mine dumps? What for?'

'To undermine me!'

We laughed raucously, sardonically.

On another occasion she said:

'Must I go with him, boys?'

'Where?'

'To the bushes near the zoo.'

'And do what there?'

'Behave like a white monkey!'

We hissed and hooted.

'He is a low beast,' Idris said.

'Don't call him a low beast,' Shireen said in mock anger.

'I said his motor-cycle is a lovely beast.'

We gathered around the motor-cycle and chanted: 'A lovely beast! A lovely beast!'

There were times Shireen failed to meet him; she was engaged in other love affairs. One night he quarrelled with her as we watched. Then he gave her presents (earrings, a watch, an engraved locket) and insisted she go with him on his motor-cycle. He pulled her by the hand. She resisted at first, then eagerly, willingly, went towards his motor-cycle, but suddenly broke free and ran into the yard. He stood beside his motor-cycle for a few minutes, thwarted, defeated. We chuckled sarcastically. He looked at us menacingly, then drove away in a torrent of gaseous noise.

Shireen told us that she had had enough of Harold and had decided to break with him. A prolonged love-affair was oppressive to her penchant for ever-varying love encounters with males. And in order to achieve the final separation she decided to spurn him in front of an audience, and we were a ready audience. She rehearsed with us her plan of action a day before.

When Harold arrived that Friday evening we clapped our hands.

'The hero is here!' Shireen shouted.

'From the gutters of Mayfair!' Nizam screamed.

Harold looked at us without saying a word. He got off his motorcycle and Shireen went towards him. We watched the two go into their usual meeting place. After a while Shireen came running towards us grouped on the opposite pavement.

'Boys, give me a kiss! Boys, give me a kiss!'

And we kissed her.

'I belong to everybody,' she declared, facing Harold. 'To everybody, you understand. That is, to blacks only, blacks only. Whites not allowed.'

She burst out laughing. She had routed Harold. He remained in the recess, caged, humiliated. Then Nizam did a foolish thing which was not part of Shireen's plan. He went towards the motor-cycle, shouted, 'Here goes!' and pushed the machine with his leg. It crashed on the street; glass shattered. When the reverberation of the impact died away we remained silent as though something ominous had occurred. We were annoyed with Nizam. His action extinguished in a moment the exquisite pleasure we were deriving from Harold's painful humiliation in our suburb. We felt we had had enough and went away.

I saw Shireen standing beside the fallen motor-cycle, in the light of the street lamp. Then she crossed the street and went towards Harold, presumably to apologize to him.

A little later we heard a scream followed by the roar of a motor-cycle. We ran towards the shoe store and found Shireen lying huddled in the doorway recess. She was crying and had blood on her mouth.

The Commandment

MOSES LIVED IN THE YARD. He was well over seventy years of age – his matted hair a bluish grey – yet his body was surprisingly resilient and strong. About ten years earlier he had been engaged by Mr Rehman to look after his many children. Before that he had worked for many years as a builder's assistant. In a mushrooming city he had helped to build homes, skyscrapers, apartment blocks and roads: pushing wheel-barrows, excavating, operating drills, blasting.

Moses enjoyed special status and privileges not given to ordinary servants, such as being allowed to eat at the kitchen table. It was his mastery of the Gujarati language (swear words and all) that elevated him. So complete was his mastery that those who heard him speak Gujarati for the first time were dumbfounded and thought that some Indian spirit had taken possession of him. In fact some people had approached Hajji Musa to explain the phenomenon, but he had dismissed them with the cryptic declaration that some things were 'too deep' for common people to know and those who tried would 'perish by evaporation'. When not looking after the children of his employer, Moses did all sorts of odd jobs for us, such as going to the shops for a trifle or collecting our dry-cleaning. He was generally liked and the children loved him.

And then, one day, came the order that Moses should leave Fords-burg. According to the order Moses was contravening the law in three respects: firstly, he had no right of domicile in an area inhabited by Indians, Coloureds and some Chinese; secondly, he was no longer a productive labour unit; thirdly, he had no document to prove that he had been born in Johannesburg. The order stated that he was an 'alien' and that he should 'go forthwith for resettlement' to his 'tribal homeland'.

At first Moses was bewildered, but the police came several times to warn him (and warn Mr Rehman that he was harbouring an alien and faced prosecution) and he came to understand the import of the order.

Its first effect on him was that he began soliloquizing in Gujarati: 'They say I must go home. Home? Yes, Transkei. And do you know what I will find there? They tell me there is a city, with real streets and real buildings. There is also a hospital for me ... '

As Moses went on speaking, the children would gather around him, and sometimes they burst into laughter when he cracked a joke about 'home'. He would wander into our homes and utter his lament and everyone felt sorry for him.

When the period given in the order had expired, the police came again and told Moses that if he did not leave willingly, he would be jailed and transported to his 'homeland' at the state's expense. Mr Rehman was given a stern warning. Moses' time was extended by a month; if after this he was still in the yard the law would take its course.

At the prospect of his enforced removal Moses' soliloquies became interminable and at times he would shout hysterically: 'They tell me I will be happy there. There are big cities there. The air is fresh too. My chief is waiting for me. O chief I am coming, O chief ... '

Everyone tried to think of a way to save him from the 'homeland': some were for concealing him; others for disguising him; others for taking him away to some place of safety. But all ideas remained ideas. Mr Rehman was his employer and nothing could be done that would not involve him as well. He did not have the heart to tell Moses to go before the police arrived. He preferred to face the consequences.

Unable to save him, people started giving Moses presents, old clothing and money. He accepted these gratefully, and spent the money feeding the children with ice-cream and sweets.

During the final week Moses no longer slept but paced all night in the yard, talking, talking, and sometimes banging on a tin drum until our nerves became brittle. And then a queer thing happened to us. We began to hate him. Vague fears were aroused in us, as though he were exposing us to somebody or something, involving us in a conspiracy – he spoke our language – threatening our existence. Indefinable feelings began to trouble us. Of guilt? Of cowardice? We wanted to be rid of him as of some unclean thing. Suddenly everyone avoided him and the children were sternly told not to go near him. Even Mr Rehman began to feel our hostility.

'I am going to my homeland,' he went on and on. 'I am going to see my chief and all my people. There are cities there! There are parks there! There are hospitals there! And there are no cemeteries there!'

When the police arrived on the appointed day they found Moses – hanging from a roof-beam in a lavatory in the yard.

Red Beard's Daughter

OF ALL RED BEARD'S DAUGHTERS Julie fetched the highest price in a marriage transaction – but she played her father a trick on her wedding-day and he never got his money. He had three other daughters who were already married. Julie was not beautiful, though her complexion was fresh and her hair long. Her father was called Red Beard because his beard was always dyed with henna. His looks gained an added fierceness from the redness of his lips and mouth through his constant chewing of paan (betel-leaf). He had never worn a Western suit in his life; he was either to be seen in a koortah or in a long coat and matching trousers made of the finest English cloth. When he was dressed, smelling of attar and with a red fez on his head, he looked like some sort of gnome. In fact he was a mild good-humoured man who loved jokes. He had never remarried after the death of his wife, but the four liabilities she had left him he turned into assets by setting a price on them.

Red Beard received a proposal for the hand of Julie from a certain Mr Ben Areff, a shopkeeper in a distant country town. He had heard of Red Beard's practice of setting a price on his daughters, but that was no deterrent as he was a fairly wealthy man. He sent his emissaries and Red Beard agreed to bestow the hand of his daughter at the price of one thousand rands. The emissaries then wanted the date for the engagement to be fixed, and Red Beard said that they could come after two weeks and drink the 'engagement sherbet' as was the custom.

Julie was happy that she was going to be married and though she was teased a great deal by her friends and neighbours about the semi-yokel who had bespoken her, she kept her sweet temper. On the appointed day she was engaged – but Mr Ben Areff did not present himself. He sent a representative who said that he was ill with influenza and had been advised by his doctor to stay at home.

After a week Julie approached her father with a request.

'I should like to see Ben Areff before ... '

'See him? What for?'

'I ... '

'All men are the same,' Red Beard said fiercely.

'Please.'

'No!'

Julie, frightened, left the room. Red Beard sat down on the settee, crossed his legs, took a paan from a nearby tray, and began to chew. Julie's request had stung him. However, after a while his anger subsided and he thought that perhaps his daughter's request was reasonable. He, too, began to feel curious about Ben Areff's appearance. Had illness really prevented him from coming to his engagement?

The next day Red Beard telephoned Ben Areff and after inquiring about his health invited him and his emissaries for lunch on the coming Sunday.

Ben Areff and his emissaries came. When Red Beard saw the man he was shocked, but said nothing. One of the emissaries explained: 'Mr Ben Areff is the son of his late father's second wife. You know in the country ... '

'I understand,' Red Beard said, calming himself again. He thought for a while, then said: 'This is going to make things difficult. You know what modern girls are. They are inclined to be fussy.'

'You are the father,' the emissary reminded him.

Ben Areff, who was wearing sun-glasses, now took them off. He was a man of average height and looked very diffident. He wasn't the sort of man to be envied. At home neither in an Indian world nor an African world, he was a derelict socially.

'I am the father,' Red Beard answered, 'but you know times have changed. Tell me, has Mr Ben Areff proposed marriage to other girls?'

'Yes,' the man answered, rather reluctantly.

'I see,' said Red Beard. 'Well,' he continued thoughtfully, 'this alters the whole picture. Mr Ben Areff is different (you understand), but if the price is right I'll see what I can do.'

The man spoke to Ben Areff and told him that it was best for him to talk to his future father-in-law.

'Please tell me how much you want?' Ben Areff asked.

Red Beard answered without hesitation:

'You can see I have no kind of work in life. I had a shop once. Give me two thousand rands in cash and I shall be satisfied.'

Ben Areff asked the principal emissary (a fat man) to go out with him and they had a long discussion. A group of women looked at the two men and among them was Julie. She had been ordered by her father to remain in a neighbour's house until she was sent for, but she had disobeyed.

Ben Areff and the fat man re-entered the house and told Red Beard that the sum of money he wanted would be paid. The emissary then wanted a date to be fixed for the wedding, but Red Beard shrewdly declined, saying that he required time to speak to his daughter.

'Don't rush things. You know what girls are today.'

After lunch Ben Areff and the emissaries left. Later Julie entered the house and her father said to her: 'He will make a good husband for you.'

'I won't marry ... '

'What?' Red Beard screamed.

'I saw him.'

'You saw him! And what is wrong with him?' he demanded.

Julie began to weep.

'Don't you question the appearance of any of Allah's creatures,' he scolded. 'He is a good man. He will look after me when I am old. Do you want to see me die of starvation?'

Julie ran out of the room.

The emissaries came again and a final agreement was reached. Red Beard – a gritty bargainer now – was to receive, in addition to the cash sum agreed upon earlier, a sum of twenty rands a month for the rest of his life.

The wedding day was fixed. Julie again expressed her opposition to the marriage, but her father's verbal outburst silenced her. The wedding preparations went forward. Julie stiffened towards everyone – including her sisters who had come to help – as though they were part of a conspiracy to marry her off. But a week before the wedding-day her mood changed; she looked happy and everything went smoothly. It seemed that she had accepted her lot.

The wedding-day arrived – but of Julie there was no sign. She had disappeared during the night. Red Beard cursed and screamed while everyone hunted for her. She had gone and left her father to face the bridegroom and the guests.

Ben Areff and his party arrived at the appointed hour. People watched him emerge from the car in the company of his relatives bearing gold jewellery and other gifts for the bride. His best man was carrying two garlands. They approached and stopped outside the house.

Red Beard was lying inside, breathing heavily as though felled by a blow. A few people took on the responsibility of telling Ben Areff that his bride had fled.

When told of Julie's perfidy, Ben Areff looked mortally embarrassed and humiliated. He stood there as if not knowing what to do. Then, he turned to his best man, took one of the garlands and hung it on the door-knob. The action fractured the tension and in some way restored his dignity. After that he and his party left.

The garland hung on the door-knob till evening. By then the flowers had withered.

Film

NOTHING, SINCE THE TIME OF THE BEARD controversy, had shaken Muslims as much as the imminent release of the film *The Prophet* on the Johannesburg cinema circuit. Though the film had received early publicity, it had not yet been seen by anyone, not even by Hermes Films, the syndicate that had bought it in America. The film was to arrive shortly by Pan American jet from Hollywood. The anger of devout Muslims was aroused and I found myself, working as a free lance journalist at the time, in the thick of the issue. A day did not pass without individuals and representatives of religious groups urging me to inform not only the cinema syndicate but the 'entire world' that the film was 'sacrilegious' and 'blasphemous' and that its screening would 'not be tolerated'.

The directors of Hermes Films approached the religious objections to the film in a secular way and stated that the decision to release the film or not could only be taken, in the rational order of things, after the film had been seen and that they would invite Muslim religious organizations to a preview. The response only served to leaven the anger of Muslims and the Islamic Academy convened a Muslim Council to deal with the matter. The Muslim Council, after a day of deliberation, decided to detail their objections in a letter to Hermes Films and gave a copy to the press. The pith of the letter read:

'You the directors of Hermes Films have invited us to sin by seeing the film. How can we, believers in the sacred Law of the Almighty, sit down with you in a den of iniquity – you will agree that cinemas are places where scenes of revelry, nudity and lewd acts are screened daily – and view something that blasphemes our Prophet Mohammed? Tractors will not pull us there, never mind oxen.

'Lest you are ignorant of the Law of Islam on picture-making, let us apprise you that all pictures of animate objects are banned, whether of pencil, paint, crayon or celluloid. Our Prophet said:

'Every picture-maker will be in the fire of Hell'. Our Prophet had foreseen the time when picture-makers, and the hosts of godless others involved in the film industry, including your good selves, would want to corrupt the virtuous people of the earth and placed a strong unequivocal injunction against pictures. It is even reported by his contemporaries that he said: 'Angels do not enter a house in which there is a dog or a picture.' So do not presume to tell us that it is rational to see something before it can be condemned. We don't have to see something that is damned from the beginning.

'You will now appreciate your own temerity in asking us to sin by viewing the film. Anyone involved with this film will be consigned to the fires of Hell even if he is an angel in every other respect.'

I went to interview Mr Winters of Hermes Films on the reaction of his syndicate to the letter. He was a big man, pale in complexion, with bronze hair cut in a fringe over his forehead. He was sitting behind a walnut-wood desk in his office on the eighteenth floor of Twentieth Century Centre.

'You will appreciate,' he said, leaning forward, with his grey eyes twinkling under bushy brows, 'that my company operates strictly on a financial basis and that all other issues are irrelevant. The film has been bought for a hundred thousand rands and we intend to release it for screening.'

'You do not think the objections have any validity?'

'None. The film, we are informed, is historically true.'

'Are you certain there is nothing offensive?'

'Nothing. The Prophet is portrayed as a hero.'

I recorded his statements in my notebook and prepared to leave.

'By the way,' he said, coming with me to the door, 'you can state in your report that cinemas are very democratic places and that no one is compelled to go to them,'

The press report of the interview outraged Muslim conscience. The film became the topic of conversation and the theme of every sermon at every mosque. The Muslim Council was summoned again and this time an aggressive tone was added to its deliberations. The Council finally decided on the types of action to be taken against the cinema syndicate if they carried out their intention to release the film: protest resolutions would be adopted by Muslim groups throughout the country and telegrams sent to the syndicate; international Muslim organizations and all Muslim governments would be urged to lodge strong protests; demonstrations would be held. As the issue was now beginning to look grave and required daily attention, an Action Committee of five men headed by Molvi Haroon was elected.

One incident marred the unanimity of the proceedings of the Muslim Council. A Mr Mohammed proposed a resolution that a telegram should be sent to the Prime Minister urging him to ban the film under the Censorship Act. Molvi Haroon immediately objected and pointing a warning index finger at Mr Mohammed said: 'The entire matter has nothing to do with politics.' Mr Mohammed retorted: 'Molvi Haroon, you should not think I am one of your pupils.' Molvi Haroon replied: 'I wish you had been, for you would then have experienced how I deal with those who are insolent.' Mr Mohammed countered with: 'You think I am an inhabitant of Lilliput!' Fortunately for Mr Mohammed, Molvi Haroon, who had not heard of that country, could not savour the innuendo and the dispute ended.

The upshot of the meeting was that Hermes Films found themselves receiving an avalanche of letters, telegrams, cablegrams and protest resolutions. I telephoned Mr Winters and asked him if there was any change in his company's attitude and he replied curtly: 'My company is not prepared to communicate with fanatics. Our intention to release the movie still stands.'

The Action Committee responded: 'We are determined to eliminate this plot of the enemies of Islam. We shall reduce to ashes Twentieth Century Centre and any cinema screening the film even if it means human sacrifice on our part.'

I telephoned Mr Winters and asked him what his company intended doing. He informed me that a meeting of the directors would take place the next day and if I came up immediately after the meeting he would give me their reply. I went the next day and while I was being whisked in the lift to the eighteenth floor it occurred to me that this would perhaps be the last time I came there as, on the next day, if Hermes Films did not capitulate, the building would be gutted by fire. I waited in the reception room – among ferns, cyclamens and begonias – for the crucial decision.

When Mr Winters entered the room looking crestfallen I knew his company had capitulated. He told me: 'My company is prepared to settle the dispute. We don't want to give Muslims the trouble of setting fire to Twentieth Century Centre and we don't want to be held responsible for giving them the opportunity of committing suicide.

They can have the film for a hundred thousand rands and hold a ceremonial burning if they wish.'

On being informed of the decision the Action Committee replied briefly: 'We regret we are unable to accept the offer of Hermes Films as it is too expensive.'

It seemed that the whole issue would now enter the doldrums of the bargaining table and the promise of the fire-cracker fuse fizzle out, since Hermes Films made no further overture. Then the film was advertised for screening at the Pantheon Cinema and the fuse flared up again.

The Action Committee hurriedly summoned a plenary session of the Muslim Council to decide on collective action. The meeting began on a stormy note when Mr Mohammed suggested that the Council in organising resistance seek the assistance of political groups. 'The film is an insult to people who are not white. Our fight against the film is a fight for freedom.' Pandemonium broke out. A dozen voices accused Mr Mohammed of introducing politics into religion. An Action Committee member shouted: 'At the last meeting you wanted the film banned and now you talk of freedom. You are nothing but an opportunist trying to take over the Council.' 'You're a liar!' Mr Mohammed roared and rushed forward to grapple with the speaker. But he fell over a chair as several men attempted to intercept him. Mr Mohammed's fall had the effect of calming everyone's tempers and Molvi Haroon went on to harangue the meeting. 'The Prophet says in the Koran: "Verily, the life of this world is but play, amusement, mutual pride and the accumulation of wealth and sons". Now is politics not part of the life of this world? Is politics not amusement, mutual pride and the accumulation of wealth?

Ibn Abbas reported ... ' Mr Mohammed jumped up from his seat and shouted: 'Why leave your five sons out?' There was pandemonium again.

The meeting ended with a declaration that trumpeted a call to arms:

'We Muslims proclaim to the enemies of Islam that the choice is between the film and our lives. Either we live and the film dies, or the film lives and we perish. The accursed progeny of Satan are operating an international conspiracy to discredit our Prophet.

'Will Muslims rise in a Jihad to defend the honour of our Prophet? The first answer has already been given by our protests. We shall finally answer with our blood which will dye the surface of the earth red.

'We call on all Muslims to join us in a march on the Pantheon for the purpose of incinerating the cinema and its owner.

'May Allah continue to guide us.'

On a Monday afternoon I went to Red Square where the demonstrators gathered. There were about a thousand men from all over the country. Some were dressed in white robes, some in Arab garb with burnouses, some sported embroidered silk turbans. They were all bearded. Molvi Haroon, looking very distinguished in a saffron-coloured turban, would lead the procession into the heart of the city and personally light the flame that would set the cinema ablaze. The Action Committee rallied the men – two standards with green flags emblazoned with the Islamic moon and star were raised aloft – and the demonstrators were about to set out when the security police arrived.

An officer came up to Molvi Haroon and a few others who were standing apart and asked them courteously if they would permit him to read a proclamation.

'What proclamation?' Molvi Haroon asked.

'Let me read it then you will all know at once.'

The Action Committee conferred together and decided that no harm would be done by allowing the proclamation to be read. In any case they were not involved in politics.

The officer motioned with his hands to everyone to come closer and read: 'You are hereby informed on this the 10th day of March, 19– , at 2.13 p.m. by me, Captain Martinus Paulus Reichman, that in terms of the Riotous Assemblies Act of 19– no meetings of persons for the purpose of public demonstrations may be held.'

When the Captain had finished Molvi Haroon smiled at him and told him with an ironic look in his eyes: 'This is a religious gathering.'

'Are you trying to tell me that you are holding a religious gathering in Red Square on a Monday afternoon? I am giving you and your people exactly fifteen minutes to disperse, otherwise my men will charge.'

The Action Committee held a quick meeting and then Molvi Haroon addressed the demonstrators, who all sat down on the ground, in Urdu. He told them that the infidels were trying to lure them into politics but they would not succeed. There was a conspiratorial crusade against Muslims, but their eventual triumph was as certain as the triumph of Saladin. Nothing would ever deter them from setting fire to the Pantheon Cinema and its owner. They should all find their way in ones and twos, using devious routes, into the city centre and gather outside the cinema.

The demonstrators felt dispirited. The appearance of the police, with guns in shining holsters, the menace of the truncheons and batons swinging playfully in their hands, was enough to cow the boldest, and many of them, instead of finding their way to the cinema found their way home. They were law-abiding citizens and did not want to get involved in politics (anything involving the security police was political). However, the Action Committee and ten others reached the Pantheon. I had preceded them in my car and waited for them to arrive. They gathered outside the cinema, a huge granite structure with a red neon sign flashing above its five entrance doors: *The Prophet*. Around massive pillars were posters in glass show cases advertising the film.

The group found themselves jostled by the pedestrians and by the people entering the cinema, and by those examining the posters. Several curious onlookers gathered to stare at the men in white robes and with ferocious beards. Some people congratulated them and expressed the hope that their presence would make the film a success (they thought that the group's presence was a gimmick by the owner of the cinema to attract the attention of the public). Others wanted to know where they came from and if they were real Arab sheiks. Children holding their mothers' hands shouted: 'Mummy! Look at their beards! Mummy! Look at their beards!' The noise of the city exploded all around them and they began to feel lost. After a while a doorkeeper in maroon uniform with gilt buttons and yellow braid, seeing the men standing for too long a period, came up to them and told them to move on as they were obstructing the pavement which had become unusually crowded with people trying to enter the cinema. 'And by the way,' he said, 'this cinema is for Europeans only.' The group looked at the infidel in contempt and said nothing. The doorkeeper went away, shrugging his shoulders. He came back in a short while, looking upset.

'The manager wants to know if you are Arabs or other Easterners?'

No one replied. Molvi Haroon smiled faintly.

'I say,' he shouted, 'don't you understand English? Are you Arabs or Indians or some other race?'

No one answered. More people began to gather.

I was standing near the group, so he turned to me.

'Can you tell me who these people are?'

'I can't tell,' I said, preferring to keep my professional neutrality.

He addressed the group again.

'I say, the manager wants to know. If you are Indians he knows the law. If you are Arabs he doesn't and will phone the lawyer to find out.

Will one of you speak?'

They gave the man a stony look.

'Speak! Speak!'

Throwing up his hands in frustration he went into the cinema. Soon he returned with the manager. More people had gathered around to witness the entertaining incident that was developing. The manager approached the group.

'Gentlemen, could you please identify yourselves.'

The group stood like statues. They were not going to talk to a man who was part of an anti-Islamic conspiracy.

'The darned whatever-they-are just want to make trouble,' the doorkeeper said irascibly.

'Not so fast, Valentino,' the manager said gently, turning to the spectators.

'Can anyone help please. Who are these gentlemen? What do they want?'

No one ventured an explanation. Besides, the men looked so fierce, with hatred smouldering in their eyes like ancient Assyrian warriors, that they were afraid to question them. But a lady, dressed in bottle-green slacks, with a string of beads around her neck, said to the manager:

'Why do you want to interfere with them?'

'I am not interfering. I am only trying to be helpful.'

'They don't need any help. Go back into your cinema. I am sure they don't want to enter your whites-only cinema.'

'You black bitch!' the doorkeeper shouted. 'Who are you to tell us?'

'Quiet Valentino!' the manager said.

The lady who was tall and lithe took a step towards the doorkeeper and dextrously smacked him across the face. 'Don't speak to me in that way,' she said.

'Bitch!' he screamed, lunging at her, but several people got in his way and the manager thrust his hand accidentally into his face.

The doorkeeper swore and tried to kick the lady, but instead kicked someone else who kicked back at him.

'Stop! Stop!' the manager pleaded desperately. 'It is only a small matter.'

People came running across from the opposite pavement. Cars came to a standstill and began hooting. The demonstrators found themselves pushed back towards the entrance doors of the cinema. People began to take sides. Some were for the lady, others for the doorkeeper. Tempers began to flare. The manager went on appealing for calm but nobody seemed to be listening to him. A fist bludgeoned the doorkeeper's face, scuffles broke out and suddenly everyone was fighting.

The police arrived and several gun shots were fired into the air. The reaction was almost immediate – the fighting stopped as though Doomsday had come. The police charged and the rioters ran helter-skelter, seeking refuge in shops, restaurants, pharmacies, hairdressers' salons and in the cinema.

I was standing beside the demonstrators who were huddled together in a niche in the porch of the Pantheon Cinema, unable to move because of the press of people, when the manager succeeded in making his way where we were.

'Gentlemen, come with me, please. I don't want you to be hurt.'

Molvi Haroon and his group were so shocked and bewildered by the tumult they had caused and the sudden arrival of the police that when the manager appeared, urging them to go with him, they felt that a saviour had come to lead them to a place of safety.

'This way, gentlemen,' the manager said, taking Molvi Haroon's hand, pushing others out of the way, leading them into the building. I followed. He shepherded us through an inner door and giving us over to usherettes with torches quickly disappeared.

The auditorium was thickly carpeted and overhead faint stars were shining in an indigo sky. We sank into plush velvet seats. On the panoramic screen a procession of Arab horsemen was approaching a desert city. It was met at the entrance gate by the chieftain who led the way to his palace where the riders dismounted. They entered a splendid room where a feast lay spread. While the handsome 'Prophet' and his party were feasting, flutes began to play and dancing girls in diaphanous jade silk glided in among the guests ...

Obsession

ONE OF GOOL'S ASSOCIATES WAS MILO, a short, stocky, well-dressed man who would come to Fordsburg in his white convertible Chrysler. As he drove past, he would greet the Indian women walking along pavements or standing on balconies, but none of them ever bothered to return his greetings.

He was a master at billiards and seldom suffered a defeat in Gool's premises in High Road. One day he said to Gool while surveying the billiard table: 'The Indian women are lovely, especially in their saris ... '

And he bent over the table arid smacked the ball with the cue. It rebounded from the end of the table, collided with another that careered straight into the net at the opposite end.

'So you are taken by the mysterious East, eh?' Gool said, chalking his cue.

'Beauty!' Milo said, moving to the other side of the table.

'They're expensive, unlike your women who are bought with cattle.'

'Expensive?'

'Gold.'

Gool thrust his stick at the ivory ball; it shot from side to side, failing to strike a red renegade on the edge.

'Gold for an Indian woman ... ' Milo said softly, steering three balls one after another into the net.

'Gool, any good Indian film showing today?'

'Not a bad one at the Lyric.'

Milo looked at his watch and said: 'Time for two more games.'

He gathered the balls and arranged them in the centre of the table.

Going to the Lyric Cinema had a double attraction for Milo. There was firstly the attraction of the female cinema-goers. He would gaze at the richly-attired women, smelling of exotic perfumes, their eyes glittering in the foyer lights, hair either coiffured or hanging in tresses, and saris sensuously exposing midriffs.

Sometimes he would be given a seat beside a woman. In the crepuscular light he would glance surreptitiously at her profile. Then there was the attraction of the film itself. Though he failed to understand the language or the plot, he feasted visually on the gorgeous film stars, their garments taut against their bodies, and jewellery embellishing their necks, wrists and ankles.

Yet, after the film-show was over and the women had passed him by as another cipher in the world of helots, a feeling of depression would constrict him. He would drive his car homewards, pass by drab barracoon-type houses, go through muddy roads skirted by dirt and poverty, and look at the women dressed in dun coarse skirts and shapeless smocks. When he reached home he would survey his wife with latent scorn as though she were an Amazon, his mind still ablaze with the feminine world of the cinema. And when he went to bed at night kaleidoscopic images of Eastern women would invade his mind, and a sense of injustice in the scheme of things, and of his own unblazoned place in it, would overwhelm him.

Medina House was a mansion, Eastern in design, form and ornamentation. One entered it from Terrace Road. There was a high wrought-iron gate flanked on either side by a wall six feet high with spikes running along the top. A flight of steps led to a portico, the columns embossed with leaves and lotuses. A large double door, the upper half consisting of mosaic glass, gave entry into a hall with several doors: one opening to the stairs that led to the upper floor of the mansion with its latticed balcony; another leading into a large living-room where a model of the Taj Mahal was prominently exhibited, and the adjoining dining room; and another to the basement room where the Darsot family's jewellery was kept in a large green safe.

The Darsots had two daughters, Noorunisha and Khalida. Noorunisha was the elder. She was a modest good-looking girl with long black hair which she plaited into two pigtails. She was naturally shy and her parents did not have to tell her not to talk to males. She had had several proposals of marriage, but her father had rejected them on the ground that the families of the suitors were not of his financial and social standing.

Milo sent Belinda, a girl friend, to seek work at Medina House. She was refused at first, but after several applications Mrs Darsot was impressed by Belinda's eagerness to serve her, and engaged her as housemaid. Belinda soon acquainted herself with the mansion and its contents and gave Milo all the particulars. Milo decided that the best time to enter Medina House would be at about ten in the morning when Mrs Darsot and her daughters would be alone. To gain entry into the mansion he devised a plan. He obtained a van and had the following words printed on the outside: York Safe Co. Ltd. With two others he drove up to the mansion and rang the bell at the gate. When Mrs Darsot came Milo said that he had been sent by his firm to deliver a small safe. Mrs Darsot, seeing the men in their work clothes and the van of the firm in the street, unlocked the gate. Milo and his men carried in a crate (containing pieces of scrap iron). Immediately they were inside the mansion they locked the door, rounded up everyone at gun-point and herded them into one room.

When Milo saw Noorunisha he was mesmerized. Prior to Milo's entry she had been preparing to go out shopping with her aunt and cousin who would be arriving to fetch her. She had had a bath, dressed herself in an elaborate gold-inwoven sari of black silk, combed her hair, and had just completed darkening her eyelids with kohl. Controlling himself Milo demanded all the money and jewellery that was kept in the safe in the basement room. Mrs Darsot agreed to give him everything. But Milo, his eyes fixed on Noorunisha, ordered the girl to take the keys and lead him to the room.

In the basement room he took the keys from her and opened the safe. The jewellery was in velvet-covered boxes. He opened a box, took several pieces and examined the filigree handiwork. Then he took a gold necklace smouldering with rubies and turning to Noorunisha – a hieroglyph of fear – placed it around her neck. Next he selected two earrings and hooked them to her pierced ear lobes. He lifted her arms and adorned her wrists with bangles and her fingers with rings. Finally, he walked around her, admiring her. Before him stood a woman miraculously come down from cinema screens, in appearance like Nargis herself, his favourite film star.

Thanking his gangster gods, Milo took Noorunisha's hand.

One of his partners came rushing down the steps. He saw Noorunisha decorated with jewellery and Milo kissing her hand.

'Milo … ? What … '

Milo awoke from an Eastern night's dream.

'Go … ? back,' he said.

The partner quickly removed the jewellery from Noorunisha and stuffed it into his pockets, saying:

'Come! Quick! There is knocking at the door.'

He grabbed Milo by the arm and the two men rushed up the stairs where they were joined by the third partner. The three, guns in hand, then opened the door and rushed out – past two shocked women – ran down the steps, jumped into their van and drove away.

In the street Noorunisha's cousin had parked his car behind the van. He had been waiting for his mother and sister who had got off to fetch her when he saw the three men emerging from the gate and hurriedly getting into the van. Realizing that they were robbers he gave chase, but after a while lost track of them. He returned to Medina House where he found everyone unhurt, and hurriedly telephoned the police.

In the speeding van Milo's partner said to him:

'What made you do that?'

'Do what?'

'Putting all that jewellery on the girl.'

'Did I?' Milo said, accelerating the van towards the Main Reef Road.

'Wasn't there any money in the safe?'

'No.'

The van's tyres screeched at a bend and sped towards Soweto.

'Look!' Milo said.
There was a police road-block ahead.

Gerty's Brother

I FIRST SAW GERTY IN A SHOP IN Vrededorp. Vrededorp, as everyone knows, is cleft in two by Delarey Street: on the one side it is colonized by us blacks and on the other side by whites. The whites come over to our side when they want to do their shopping, and return with a spurious bargain or two. I saw her in a shop in the garishly decorated Indian shopping lane called Fourteenth Street. I had gone there with my friend Hussein who wanted to see a shopkeeper friend of his. I think the shop was called Dior Fashions, but of that I am not quite sure because shop follows shop there and this one didn't strike me as being in any way fashionable. Anyway, that is where I saw her. My friend spoke to the shopkeeper – a fat dark man with a darker moustache – and I just looked around and smoked a cigarette.

I sat down on a chair and then I noticed two figures darken the doorway and enter the shop, a girl and a boy. The shopkeeper spoke to the girl and then suddenly laughed. She laughed too, I think. I wouldn't have taken any further notice of the group as I was seated at the back of the shop. But then the shopkeeper switched to Gujarati and spoke to my friend. I heard him say that she was easy and would not give much trouble in removing her undergarments to anyone, but one had to be careful as there was the usual risk involved. Hussein replied that he was keen and wouldn't like to waste much time about the matter. I think the shopkeeper introduced him to her at this stage. Then I heard him telling Hussein that he was going to organize a dance at his place on the following Saturday evening, that he was going to invite Gerty, and that if Hussein was interested he could take her away from his place. All this he said in Gujarati, rather coarsely I thought.

Later, when Hussein and I had climbed into his Volkswagen and were on our way to Fordsburg, he informed me that to soften her before the party on Saturday he had bought the girl a frock. He asked me how I liked her and I said she was all right as far as I was concerned, though, of course, I had not been near enough to see her properly and size her up. But I said she was all right and he felt very satisfied at having bumped into a white girl. He told me that she lived in Vrededorp, 'on the other side', and that she seemed to be very easy. He said that when he had done with her he would throw her over to me and I could have her as well. I answered with a vague 'Let the time come'. He then said something about 'pillar to post', and laughed as the car tore its way through the traffic into Fordsburg.

Saturday night I was at my landlady's, stripped to the waist because of the heat, reading an old issue of *The New Statesman*. There was a knock on the door and somebody asked for me and entered. It was Hussein all dressed up with bow tie and cuff-links and gleaming shoes that were out of place in my spartan room.

'Where to, my dandy friend?' I asked admiringly.

'To the dance party. I thought you would be ready. You promised to come with me.'

I said I had forgotten, but that I would be ready in a minute. I dressed quickly, but didn't care to put on a white shirt or a tie. I wasn't very particular about what I wore and I think it pleased my friend because my appearance was something of a foil to his, and set off to advantage his carefully put-together looks.

We set off in his Volkswagen for Vrededorp and in a few minutes the car braked sharply in Eleventh Street in front of the house of Hussein's shopkeeper friend. We were quite early and there were not many people present. Hussein's friend was happy to see us and he introduced us to those who were there. There were some lovely-looking girls in shimmering coral and amber and amethyst-coloured saris and others in more sober evening dresses.

After a while Hussein asked to see the shopkeeper privately, and I think they went out to the front verandah of the house. When they returned I saw that Hussein was not too pleased about something or other. Other girls arrived, all gaily dressed and very chic and charming and I was beginning to look forward to a swinging evening. The girls offered me tea and cake and other tasty things to eat and I didn't refuse as my boarding-house wasn't exactly a liberal establishment. All this time my friend Hussein was walking in and out of the room, and was on the look-out whenever someone knocked on the door and entered the house. The party got going and we danced, ate the refreshments provided and talked some euphonious nonsense.

I was just getting interested in a girl, when my friend interrupted me and said that he wanted to see me urgently. I followed him and we went to the verandah. Someone had switched off the lights and I saw two figures standing there, a girl and a small boy. He introduced her to me as Gerty. He then took me aside and asked me if I could drive the two of them to the Zoo Lake immediately and leave them in the park for a while, and if I could keep her brother company while he saw to Gerty's needs. As it was a risky business he didn't want the others in the party to know. He would like to get done with it before joining the party.

I said I didn't mind and the four of us got into the car. I drove to the Lake. It was a lovely night in December and we breathed in the luminous wind of the city streets as the car sped along. Hussein and Gerty sat in the back seat. They didn't say much to each other, but I guessed that they were holding hands and fondling. Gerty's brother sat beside me. He must have been seven or eight, but I didn't take much notice of him. He was eating some cakes and chocolates that Hussein had taken from the house. I dropped the pair in a park near the Lake. Hussein asked me to return in about an hour's time. The park was a darkness of trees and lawns and flowers, and it occurred to me that it made no difference if one slept with a white or a black girl there.

Gerty told her brother that he mustn't worry and that she was all right and that he should go with me for a while. Before I drove off he asked me what they were going to do and I said they must be a bit tired and wanted to rest, but that did not sound convincing. Then I said that they had something to discuss in private and the best place was in the park. He agreed with me and I started the car. I didn't feel like driving aimlessly about for an hour so I drove towards the lake. I asked the boy what his name was and he said Riekie.

I parked the car under some pine trees near a brightly-lit restaurant. There were people dining on the terrace amid blaring music, others were strolling on the lawns or resting on the benches. I asked Riekie if he would like an ice-cream and took him to the restaurant and bought him one. We went down to the water's edge. The lake is small with an islet in the middle; a fountain spouted water into shifting rays of variegated light. Riekie was fascinated by it all and asked me several questions.

I asked him if he had ever sat in a boat. He said he hadn't. I took him to the boat-house and hired one. The white attendant looked at me for a moment and then at Riekie. I knew what he was thinking about but I said nothing. He went towards the landing-stage and pointed to a boat. I told Riekie to jump in, but he hesitated. So I lifted him and put him into the boat. He was light in weight and I felt the ribs under his arms. A sensation of tenderness for the boy went through me. You must understand that this was the first time I had ever picked up a white child.

I rowed out towards the middle of the lake, and went around the fountain of kaleidoscopic lights. Riekie was gripped by wonder. He trailed his hands in the cool water smelling of rotted weeds, and tried to grab the overhanging branches of the willows along the banks.

It was time to pick up Hussein and Gerty. Riekie looked disappointed, but I said I would bring him there again. At this he seemed satisfied and I rowed towards the landing-stage.

Hussein and Gerty were waiting for us. They got into the car and we returned to the party in Eleventh Street,

The party was now in full swing. There were many girls and I didn't waste much time. My friend stuck to Gerty, and if he was not dancing with her he was talking to her. And by the time the party ended at midnight Riekie had fallen asleep on a sofa and had to be doused with water to wake him.

We dropped Gerty and her brother at a street corner on our way to Fordsburg. Hussein had rooms of his own in Park Road, situated in a small yard at the end of a passage. A tall iron gate barred the entrance to the passage. There were only three rooms in the yard. Hussein occupied two and the other was occupied by a decrepit pensioner who lived in his room like some caged animal, except that no one ever came to see him.

At first Hussein was afraid to tell Gerty where he lived. There was the usual risk involved. But I think eventually he came to the conclusion that in life certain risks had to be taken if one was to live at all. And so Gerty and her brother came to his rooms and she took on the role of mistress and domestic servant and Riekie became the pageboy.

Gerty and Riekie were very fond of each other. The harsh realities of life – they were orphans and lived in poverty with an alcoholic elder brother – had entwined them. Hussein didn't mind Riekie's presence. In fact the boy attached himself to him. My friend was generous, and besides providing Gerty with frocks for summer, he bought the boy clothing and several pairs of shoes. Riekie was obedient and always ready to run to the shops for Hussein, to polish his shoes or wash the car. In time his cheeks began to take on colour and he began to look quite handsome. I noticed that he wasn't interested in boys of his own age; his attachment to his sister seemed to satisfy him.

Riekie would often come to my landlady's in the company of Hussein, or my friend would leave him there when he had some business with Gerty. If I was in the mood to go to the movies I would take him with me.

And then things took a different turn. Hussein came to understand that the police had an eye on him, that somehow they had come to know of Gerty and were waiting for an opportunity to arrest him in incriminating circumstances. Someone had seen a car parked for several nights near his rooms and noticed the movements of suspicious-looking persons. And he was convinced the police were after him when one night, returning home late, he saw a man examining the lock of the gate. As he was not in the mood for a spell of prison, he told her that she should keep away from him for some time, and that he would see her again as soon as things were clear. But I think both of them realised that there wasn't much chance of that.

There wasn't much that one could tell Riekie about the end of the affair. My friend left it to Gerty, and went to Durban to attend to his late father's affairs.

One Sunday morning I was on my way to post some letters and when I turned the corner in Park Road there was Riekie, standing beside the iron gate that led to my friend's rooms. He was clutching two bars with his hands, and shouting for Hussein. I stood and watched as he shouted. His voice was bewildered.

The ugly animal living in the yard lurched out of his room and croaked: 'Goh way boy, goh way white boy. No Hussein here. Goh way.'

Riekie shook the barred gate and called for Hussein over and over again, and his voice was smothered by the croaks of the old man.

I stood at the corner of the street, in my hand the two letters I intended to post, and I felt again the child's body as I lifted him and put him into the boat many nights ago, a child's body in my arms embraced by the beauty of the night on the lake, and I returned to my landlady's with the hackles of revolt rising within me.

Ten Years

YASMIN, A GIRL OF ABOUT FIFTEEN, was in her bedroom seated on her bed, sobbing. After she had returned from the court in the afternoon, she had locked herself in her room, refusing to allow her father or anyone else – her aunts and cousins and hordes of other sympathisers – to enter the room.

It was now past six in the evening. The street lights in the narrow smoke-filled streets of Fordsburg were glowing. Yasmin's father, Mr Adam Suleiman, the veteran Orient Front politician, was in the lounge of their small house, reading the evening paper. For the second time now he was reading the report of the trial, the final summing up of the case by the judge, the verdict, and the sentences passed on the five men found guilty of sabotage. Their photographs were prominently displayed, but he focused his eyes on one face only – his son's face, passionless like a mask, carved in deep shadows.

'Ten years, ten years,' he whispered feebly, and he felt, with a painful finality, the closing of a shutter somewhere inside him.

The arrest and trial of his son Amin had racked him. The protracted, involved court proceedings, the endless discussions with the counsel for the defence, the expense, the anxiety – these had corroded his health and mental composure. He looked like an ascetic, an ascetic who had failed to find the promised bliss.

At seven his eldest son Ebrahim was to arrive from Durban. There was some comfort in having another son. Although he would no longer have his favourite son near him, he hoped that Ebrahim would decide to stay with him and be a buttress to him in the years of anguish that faced him.

Mr Adam Suleiman's political experience included the rigours of prison life. He had been imprisoned several times during his long politically active career; every time the Orient Front had embarked on a passive resistance campaign against some discriminatory law or other, he had been in the forefront. The campaigns had ended without achieving anything much to speak of. But now in retrospect he felt thankful: he would be closer to his son's anguish during his long period of incarceration.

At seven Ebrahim arrived. Father and son greeted each other, but rather coldly. Ebrahim sat down on a chair, and after a few moments of strained silence, jolted his father by saying, 'So he had to join the saboteurs. I suppose he became desperate.'

Mr Adam Suleiman scanned his son's face; he looked there for some softness, some mellow sympathetic quality. But on Ebrahim's astringent face there was only implacability and bitter scorn. There was no trace of pity for a brother imprisoned for ten years.

'I don't understand what you mean,' the father said in a timid voice.

'Don't you?' Ebrahim asked with ironic emphasis.

'No. I don't.'

Ebrahim produced a packet of cigarettes from his pocket, and, with his dark bony fingers, lit one.

'So you don't grasp what I mean? Must I clarify to you the stupidity of his action and the stupidity of your encouragement – the crass imbecility of it all. Blowing up pylons and all that!'

'There is no point in talking about the past. Your brother is in prison.'

There was anger within the father, but anaemic and muted. He hated his son just then for smoking nonchalantly as if nothing had happened. And Ebrahim had not even cared to inquire about his sister. She was still in her room, but no longer crying.

'And why should I not talk about it at all? Are you trying to forget the past? Do you expect me to forget the time when you told me to leave this house because you could not stand my politics and my ideas? You forget the quarrels in this house.'

'I have not forgotten them. But please forget the past at the present moment. Have you no feelings for your brother?'

'Is it my fault – the ten years? Or his own? Or yours perhaps?'

'My fault? What do you mean? In what way am I responsible for his imprisonment?'

'I suppose I must enlighten you. You seem to have a short memory.

Do you forget your unreasoned defence of the stupidities perpetrated by the Orient Front and your unfatherly rages when I refused to be your flunkey and follower?'

'O forget the past, my son. I cannot bear to think of it.'

'And do you forget that you told me to leave this house when you were afraid that Amin was beginning to see the absurdity of your politics and was on the point of joining the People's Movement?'

The father did not answer.

'And now that Amin is in prison and you need me you have sent for me. I suppose you think I have no kind of human dignity and self-respect; you can pick me up and throw me away as you will.'

Mr Suleiman remained silent.

'Do you admit that you were wrong in your politics, and that you wronged me by ordering me to leave this house?'

Mr Suleiman did not reply. There was an inner resistance to admitting this. He feared that his son would quickly seize upon the admission in order to make satirical invasions into the past.

'You do not admit because to face reality is too much for you. You supported the Orient Front in its time (I need not remind you that most of the leaders have now absconded from the country) and the few remaining supporters – like my brave brother Amin – are in desperation blowing up the doors of a post office here, a pylon there, or a pillar or two of some public building. The Herrenvolk laugh at your childish actions and gather you with ease into their nets. But what can one expect from fools of the first order. Need I remind you of what happened to your passive resistance campaigns? You called me a traitor, a coward. And what did you achieve? Nothing. No, perhaps not nothing, but a kick from the Herrenvolk jackboot and a taste of prison life.'

'Perhaps you are right. But you seem to forget that we were brave and dared, while you sat, critical, inactive, afraid.'

'Yes, but what about the futility of your actions? You seem to forget that Amin has been given ten years. Ten years for daring, for being brave as you call it.' Action without the possibility of achieving anything – that is not audacity but stupidity and rashness.'

The father bowed his head.

'And you encouraged Amin to join the band of desperate men. You are responsible for his imprisonment. Yes, you can now go and scribble, as you used to do, on public buildings: 'Down with tyrants', 'Down with the Group Areas Act', 'Freedom is around the corner' and so forth. Such scribbling may sooth your conscience, make you feel that your cause is exalted, that you are contributing to the liberatory struggle. But all your life you have fed yourself on delusions. My mother – you dragged her from one prison to another on your senseless passive resistance campaigns. Her illness did not matter to you – the cause was more important. At her death your grief was a travesty; you gloated at what people said about her being a martyr, a woman who had dedicated her life to the cause of freedom. You were blind to the obvious insincerity of their words. And what has happened to your philosophy of non-violence, the Gandhian principles that you and your Front professed to uphold? Passive resistance! A contradiction in terms, that is what it is. Political suicide and political madness, the way of the weak and the cowardly. And when passive resistance failed after the Herrenvolk courts had kicked you enough in the guts, you and your Front turned in panic to perform ineffectual puerile gestures – blowing up pillars and pylons. Just as little children, unable to punish a parent who frustrates them, resort to breaking up their playthings. You have always lived in a world of delusions, with Utopia to be purchased around the corner.'

Mr Adam Suleiman wilted under the blast of accusatory words. He felt defeated and humbled, his life crumbling within him. He would have infinitely preferred a spell in prison to the venomous tongue of his son. At a time when he ardently needed commiseration, the futility of his whole political life was forced on him.

And then his daughter's bedroom door opened. She stood before them, her long black hair dishevelled and flowing over her green dress, her eyes reddened by crying. She was like some figure in a tragedy, lacerated by the political passions that were a part of her family.

Ebrahim rose, went towards her, touched her head with his hand – and then promptly left the house.

In Two Worlds

I FIRST MET HENRY LEVIN THE DAY I went to the Witwatersrand University to attend a lecture by an American professor of Political Science who had been invited by the Humanist Association of which Henry was the chairman. The lecture centred round the twin subjects of patriotism and nationalism and the dangers inherent in their extreme forms: making their appeal to the herd instincts and the psychology of mob behaviour in man, they lead to the transformation of men into stereotyped personalities governed by conformity and psychopathic sadism and aggression. The answer to the dangers of patriotism and fascism was humanism ...

After the lecture a friend introduced me to Henry. In appearance he was tall, sinewy, with soft blond hair and azure eyes. By temperament he seemed to be a warm friendly person. He invited us to his home where there was to be a small party and we went along with a few others.

Some time later I met him again. He informed me that he had completed his studies in Political Science at the University and hoped to leave for Oxford in a few months' time. I suggested that if he was not involved in any work he could be of assistance at a private school where I was teaching. He agreed and the next day he came to the school.

Henry experienced no difficulty in adapting himself to his role as a teacher. His approach to teaching, being neither pedantic nor authoritarian, quickened in pupils their potentialities of intellectual curiosity, self-expression and creativity. And after school he organized debates and study groups to encourage pupils to respond critically to their social, political and economic environment.

Henry's parents lived in Sandown. On several occasions I accompanied him to his home, but I found the atmosphere of the suburb with its avenues of trees and solitary mansions amid acres of gardens, chilling. It lacked the noise – the raucous voices of vendors, the eternal voices of children in streets and backyards – the variety of people, the spicy odours of Oriental foods, the bonhomie of communal life in Fordsburg. And it was not long before Henry too was attracted by our way of life. He became part of our intense way of living, our inordinate interest in the affairs of our fellow beings whom we could summon with a shout or with the knock of a shoe against a shared wall. He made many new friends and often would not go home at all for several days.

I introduced him to a political group, the Capricorn Society, an affiliate of the People's Movement. After he had attended several meetings and come to understand its principles and objectives, he decided to join it. Meetings of the Society were held either at the school or in the home of one of the members.

Our Society's affairs began to take up much of Henry's spare time: there were meetings to attend, pamphlets to be written, journeys to undertake and historical research to be tackled. Then there was the secret, always dangerous, activity of awakening people to political consciousness. In Fordsburg Henry found an exciting way of life that went beyond that of the stagnant world of Sandown and the University's campuses and corridors. As a consequence he became an exile from home.

His parents became alarmed at his absence. They telephoned him and pleaded that he should come home, but, rather impatiently, he told them that he had new urgent responsibilities that prevented his return. In desperation his mother telephoned me and told me in a tearful aggrieved voice:

'Please don't keep Henry away.'

I spoke to Henry. His reply was uncompromising:

'I cannot go on talking about freedom and at the same time go on living among the whites. Either I live in Fordsburg or I live in Sandown.'

I was feeling uneasy about the rift between Henry and his parents. So I urged him to go home and explain to them. After a while he agreed and telephoned his parents.

He insisted that I go with him. His parents were waiting in the lounge. They were a little surprised when they saw me, but said nothing. They looked tense and nervous. His mother was a small woman, with long eyelashes and a doll-like face. His father was a well-dressed corpulent man, with a pink balding head and thick-rimmed spectacles.

'Henry,' his mother began hesitantly, 'your father and I are very worried about you.'

'Worried, mother? What for?'

'We don't see enough of you,' his father said tactlessly.

'And what do you want to see me for?'

The sudden brusque tone shocked and frightened his father. He placed his hand on his forehead and looked at his feet.

'Henry, you have a home,' his mother said softly, pleadingly. 'You cannot ... ' She looked at me and did not say what she had in mind.

I realized that my presence would not help Henry and his parents to come to an understanding; so I went out of the lounge into the garden and then walked slowly towards the car. Later Henry came and said: 'Let's go.'

As we entered the car his mother came hurriedly towards us, shouting: 'Wait Henry! Wait!'

But he shut the door and drove away. I looked back and saw a small figure on the driveway, with hands uplifted appealingly.

In the car he told me that he had informed his parents of his political commitments. And he had also told them that he would not be going on to Oxford as he would have to use their 'parasitically acquired wealth'.

When the members of the Capricorn Society came to hear of Henry's decision to separate himself from the white world he was warmly commended. There was his clear grasp of principles and single-minded allegiance to a cause that distinguished him from the mere sympathizer, the liberal who, living in some affluent suburb, periodically indulged in conscience-soothing verbal brickbats at the white establishment. Henry was one of us, living among us, with the threat of arrest ever present.

But as time went on I sensed that despite his absolute commitment to the black world and its strivings, he was beginning to be profoundly affected by his rift with his parents. On several occasions I found him in a pensive mood. One day I suggested that he should go home occasionally.

'I can't,' he answered, 'I'd betray myself if I returned.'

Then the Arab-Israeli war broke out and turmoil erupted in Jewish hearts. Henry enlisted immediately.

'Jews have suffered oppression enough,' he told me in explanation. 'I cannot stand idle and see Israel destroyed.'

I drove him to the airport where he was to join a group of volunteers. In the car he was silent and kept his eyes focused on the flitting landscape. He seemed no longer his usual self and I began to feel a subtle chord of estrangement. But I dismissed it as being part of the war hysteria that grips people, when the ego wilts and personal relations slacken.

Before he boarded the plane he told me:

'Let my parents know that I have left.'

He looked disturbed; his voice wavered. He turned and walked away quickly.

As I stood on the balcony of the airport building and looked towards the silver-blue Israeli jet standing serenely on the runway, it occurred to me that although Henry had rejected the world of his parents he had suffered the agonies of an exile while living amongst us and that his decision to go to Israel was perhaps rooted in a subconscious impulse to re-unite his divided self on national soil.

After the war Henry returned, full of breezy enthusiasm to get on with the local battle. But the Capricorn Society summoned him to a meeting to explain his action in going to Israel. Henry was bewildered; he failed to see in what way he had transgressed. The meeting was held one evening in a classroom at school. The indictment was delivered by Ntembu, our secretary:

'Gentlemen, what I have to say to you this evening is in no way motivated by any personal feelings. Our organization is founded on certain basic principles and tenets, and whenever anyone proves false to these, by word or by action, he can no longer remain with us.

'One of our members, Mr Henry Levin, has, by going to the assistance of Israel during the recent Middle-East conflict, flouted a basic principle of our Society. What principle? Let me explain. He has, by identifying himself with a national state, displayed the spirit of a partisan for a racial group. In our organization there are neither Jews nor Gentiles, Asians nor Coloureds, Whites nor Blacks. There are only people. We are totally opposed to the forces that seek to label, categorise and separate us racially and nationally. We place our faith in humanism and rationalism. By going to the assistance of Israel Mr Henry Levin is guilty of violating our cardinal principle. Let me ask you, gentlemen, why he did not go to assist the Vietnamese in their struggle against the Americans? The answer is that he placed national loyalty above human loyalty.

'More seriously, I contend that Mr Henry Levin, by his action, has identified himself with the oppressor's belief in Apartheid. You are all aware of the ideological dogma that there will be peace on earth and goodwill to all men when every race has its own ghetto ... '

'No!' Henry cried in an agonized voice. He stood up to speak. But words failed him.

A few minutes of uneasy silence followed during which the agony of his situation seemed to register in everyone's consciousness, his desolation amid two worlds, the world he had rejected and the world that rejected him. Moved by an impulse of collective pity, we walked out of the room silently, as though afraid to disturb him.

Labyrinth

'SAY GOOD-BYE, SAY GOOD-BYE TO PAPA,' Gool said to his three-year-old daughter. She laughed as he tickled her.

'Where you going, papa?'

'To see friends, Nazli.'

He tickled her again and she laughed again as his wife came up to him. He handed her the child. He kissed them both and then went out of the house at the rear. He entered his sports car standing in the driveway, a red Farina Spider, and drove to the street edge. His wife and child were waving at him from the door and he waved back. He looked along both sides of the street, turned left and stormed away.

He drove to High Road.

A game of billiards was in progress.

'Any news,' he asked Faizel who was chalking his cue.

'None.'

And Faizel continued playing.

There was a time, Gool remembered, when everyone there would have greeted him eagerly. Now there was a mood of sullenness enhanced by the uninterrupted clicks of colliding billiard-balls.

Gool went over to Hamid, touched him on the shoulder and took him aside.

'Everything quiet?'

'Everything quiet.'

'Keep the guns loaded.'

'They won't come in here.'

'No, but keep the guns loaded.'

When the billiards game was over Gool was offered a stick. He declined. He sat down at a table and poured some liquor into a glass from a decanter. As he sat drinking he reflected on their estrangement from him. He had been unable to counter successfully a challenge that had confronted him and his failure was leading to the psychical disintegration of the gang. 'They are deserting me,' he said bitterly to himself as he saw them clustered around the billiard-table in silent preoccupation with the game. His agony was that of a leader who finds himself rejected. Their rejection was not on a level of clear consciousness, but rather a subtle instinctive movement away from him as he could no longer lead them and offer them security.

Trouble had started when a new gang, The Spears, visited the various gambling clubs 'protected' by Gool and offered superior 'protection'. A few timorous ones among the club-proprietors had accepted the new rulers; the brave ones who dared to resist found themselves beaten up and their coffers ransacked.

The action of The Spears represented a crisis in Gool's life. He had lorded it over others for so long that his sovereignty seemed eternal. A few individuals, in earlier years, who had tried to oppose him had been silenced without much trouble. But the arrival of The Spears brought him face to face with an organized rival body. Yet it was not so much the actual physical challenge that shook him but the fact that it was possible. Physically audacious, he could oppose threat with threat, fist with fist, and bullet with bullet. But rationally and emotionally, he could not accept the possibility of a body of men deliberately banding together to subvert his rule. And neither could he accept the harsh and bitter irony of his situation; The Spears had appeared on the gangland scene at a time when, having loaded his bank coffers, he felt secured for life. At this mellow hour of repletion, their appearance enervated him and dulled his retaliative faculties. Yet, while they existed he could not look the world in the face and meet it on his own terms.

Eventually he had decided to have it out with his rivals as he could no longer bear the humiliation. He made an ostensible peace offer. He sent a message: if they would come to High Road he would be prepared to make an arrangement with them. The Spears, feeling flattered at Gool's apparent capitulation, accepted the offer and four men turned up to confer with him. The conference soon degenerated into a battle of foul words, fisticuffs – and bullets. Gool intended killing one or two of his antagonists on his own premises (he would plead self-defence as a motive later). But the ruse did not work. The Spears escaped with injuries.

It was during this melee that a bullet fired by Gool shattered the head of an alabaster statuette of Apollo and sent it crashing to the floor. The death of the god triggered an ominous reverberation through him, like seismic disorder, and in the moment's hesitation that followed his adversaries escaped. He picked up the shattered pieces, put them in a cardboard box which he left on the table-pedestal where the god had once stood. The next day he threw the box and its contents in the garbage can in the backyard.

Gool had acted unwisely in making his peace overture, for it implicitly contained his fears (though it displayed his cunning). His response and its consequences were personally disastrous for him for they fissured the bond that tied him to his gang. Had he been able to summon the selfless audacity of his former years and flung himself into the contest boldly, even at the risk of having his gang annihilated, his men would have followed him and perished gladly.

Akbar entered. Gool called him over.

'Brandy?'

Akbar sat down on a chair, but declined a drink.

'Have you heard anything?'

'No.'

'They are not planning anything?'

'I haven't heard.'

That the confrontation would come Gool knew. After the failure of his tactical defensive manoeuvre, his adversaries had retreated, but would soon show themselves. Akbar had spoken to friends all over the suburb, even posted spies. On the information gained, he would parry the enemy.

'Shall we go to the Avalon this evening?'

'Fine.'

'Let's go for the tickets now.'

'Going to the Avalon,' Akbar said loudly to the billiard-players.

Faizel joined them.

Gool drove his car to the Avalon Cinema. He parked his car near the cinema and Akbar went to get the tickets. Gool kept his car engine idling. Akbar came back.

'The cashier says he wants money.'

'Tell that fat pig since when do we pay.'

Akbar went back.

Since the advent of The Spears his status in society had shifted from its apogee. He sensed this from the attitude of people, in the way they spoke to him. A certain intonation had been elided from their speech. But he had not encountered the truculent arrogance displayed by the cinema cashier before. Had he transferred his allegiance? He realized that some people were secretly relishing his inability to annihilate his rivals, and others waiting anxiously for the final confrontation.

Suddenly a black Chrysler appeared beside Gool's car and levelled guns began spouting bullets. Gool drove away at high speed, dashed past a red traffic light, rounded several corners daringly, mounting the pavements with screaming tyres, passed a stop street without slackening, and steered his car towards the Main Reef Road. He accelerated the Spider as it weaved through the traffic, and looked into the rear-view mirror to see the pursuing car. He shouted to his companion on the back seat: 'Faizel! Faizel!' Faizel lay slumped, then groaned and Gool shouted again as he pressed the accelerator, narrowly missing a pedestrian crossing the road. His pursuers overtook several cars by hooting fiercely and they were now behind him, hooting. 'Bastards! Bastards!' Gool cried as his car engine thundered. There was a string of stationary cars ahead of him. A red light! He swerved his car to the left and sped along the gravel side road. The Chrysler still followed him. 'Swines! Swines!' he shouted, overwhelmed by their tenacious devilry. The light turned green as he reached it and he swerved in front of a car to get on the tarmac. He must get off the Main Reef Road and head towards the mine dumps, the golden mounds of sterile sand that lay on his left. Among the web of roads of Crown Mines he would be able to elude his pursuers.

He turned off the Main Reef Road. They were still following him closely. Then he saw the faces of his pursuers in the rear-view mirror: intent, grim, menacing. He turned to the right and sped down an incline, skirting a sand pyramid. His car flashed along an arc in the road, then he was over a bridge and among an avenue of trees. The road turned left, then left again. The hooter of the car behind burst into sustained tumultuous bellowing. 'Swines! Swines!' The sound stampeded in his flaming cranium. A gang of helmeted miners looked at him in a cinematic succession of facial amazement. He was in a labyrinth of arcs, tangents, radii, perimeters, alive with hideous bellowing, screaming, thundering. A sooty monster loomed and passed siren-shrieking, with gnashing pistons. A huge black door barred his way, then metamorphosed miraculously into blue ether. Faizel made a final effort to resurrect himself from the blood-stained seat at the rear, put his hand on Gool's shoulder and collapsed with a cry. The touch, like a macabre caress, and the death cry unnerved Gool. He turned his car into a sand road – the road rushed towards him then treacherously dissolved. The red Spider careered into a mantle of dust, slithered and slewed, with its engine roaring, suddenly rolled over several times and plunged down an incline, scattering sprays of yellow dust into the air, and, coming to rest at the foot of a cypress tree, exploded into an inferno.

The Notice

THE TIME CAME WHEN HOUSES were being expropriated in a section of Fordsburg and Indians pressed to go to Lenasia, a reservation some twenty miles away. When Mr Effendi's house was expropriated, he knew that the official would soon come with the usual six months' notice. But Mr Effendi decided to evade formal acceptance of the notice for several reasons: firstly, he had been coerced into selling the house; secondly, he was not happy to live in a reservation outside metropolitan Johannesburg; and thirdly, the houses in the expropriated section, according to newspaper reports, were not going to be demolished until the government authorities had finally decided on details of the Oriental Bazaar that was to be erected, and this would take two or three years.

It was easy for Mr Effendi to evade receiving the notice for he was a commercial traveller. Whenever the official came his wife would say: 'Mr Effendi he not home. He in country.'

'And when will he come home?'

'Well, he traveller. He busy man.'

And the official would depart to return on another day. But he never found Mr Effendi at home, for he always returned, whenever he did, at night and left at an early hour in the morning. At last the official became desperate as his seniors were beginning to believe that he was failing in his duty. He decided to call on Mr Effendi at night.

'Who dare?' his wife asked.

'Mr Hill. I want to speak to your husband.'

'He not home. He still in country.'

'I want to enter the house and see.'

'You can't.'

'I shall call the police if you don't let me in.'

'Au-right, I open. Wait, I go dress.'

She went to her bedroom for a while and then returned to open the door. She was a well-nourished woman in a pink gown with her plaited hair liberally oiled. The official entered the lounge and then went into the adjoining bedroom. He saw a form covered with blankets.

'Is that your husband in bed?'

Mrs Effendi looked abashed.

'I only woman and sometimes I lonely woman. Dat not my husban but friend.'

She smiled and coyly looked away as though embarrassed by the confession of marital infidelity. The official was taken aback. He walked into the lounge and Mrs Effendi followed him.

'I only woman, you understand. My husban always in country.'

The official smiled. And as an idea came into his mind, the disappointment he felt in not finding Mr Effendi at home evaporated. He went towards the door.

'You are a clever woman, Mrs Effendi. Enjoy yourself. Good night.'

Mrs Effendi closed the door, went to her bedroom and saw her husband – a hairy, fleshy, big-boned man – emerging from under the blankets.

'A stupid official! A stupid official!' he boomed between intervals of mocking guffaws. His pleasure at tricking the official was spiced by the satisfaction of defeating, though in a small way, those who had expropriated his house.

The next day the official came again. He spoke in such a friendly way that Mrs Effendi invited him into the house and offered him coffee.

'You know Mrs Effendi,' he said, settling down in an arm-chair, 'Indians are not at all bad people. They have these big shops in Market Street and they give a lot of credit.'

'Is dat so, Mr Hill?'

'Yes, I am beginning to like them.'

'Sometimes Indian people not so good. My husban sell dem goods and den dey don pay. Derefore he all de time in country.'

'That is true. That keeps him busy. And that keeps you busy too,' he added with a wink.

'You are a good man, Mr Hill, if you keep it a secret.'

'Don't worry. I can hold my tongue.'

When the official left, Mrs Effendi felt that she had him well under control and as long as this was the case she and her husband would be able to lengthen their stay in Fordsburg.

And then the official called again one night.

'I have to carry out my duty,' he said apologetically as he stepped into the lounge. Mrs Effendi let the official in as it was late and she did not expect her husband back. The official placed his bag on the table, sat on a chair and pointed at the bedroom door with a smile.

'Is he in?'

'No, he still in country.'

'I mean … you know who.'

'Oh,' she said laughing. 'No, he not come tonight. He stay wit wife.'

'Oh, he is a married man,' the official said with emphasis. He laughed merrily. 'I like you, Mrs Effendi. You are a clever woman.'

'All Indian women clever,' Mrs Effendi thanked him, smiling at his gullibility.

'Yes, they are very clever.'

Mrs Effendi excused herself and went to the kitchen to make coffee. The official now removed his jacket and lit a cigarette. When she returned with the coffee he thanked her and said: 'You know what I have done for you, Mrs Effendi? I have told the office that Mr Effendi has gone to India for a visit.'

'Really Mr Hill? Den we stay longer here?'

'Yes. It is a risk. But I am doing this only for you.'

'I very glad Mr Hill.'

'Remember, only for you. Not a word to anyone.'

'Thank you, Mr Hill.'

Mr Hill drank his coffee. Then he rose from his chair and boldly went to sit beside Mrs Effendi on the settee. She was shocked, tried to rise, but Mr Hill had his arm around her shoulders. However, after a brief struggle, she managed to free herself and went quickly to the kitchen.

He was unperturbed by Mrs Effendi's unwillingness to succumb. Perhaps she needed a little time to adjust to his transformation from an official into a Romeo. He had the night to himself and decided not to hurry matters. He saw a bowl of fruit on the table and helped himself. He munched an apple while gazing at a silver-framed picture of the Taj Mahal. 'Beautiful! Beautiful!' he whispered as a feeling of being involved in some Eastern romantic adventure – with harems of princesses, tambourines, sherbet and all that – took hold of him (he had had two double brandies in the bar shortly before his arrival). Soon a houri, clad in silk and glittering with jewels would appear before him (he had seen such things happening in films) to offer him her dusky charms. Then he ate a peach, two bananas and some grapes. After that a sense of delicious euphoria filled him. It was a sultry night. He removed his tie, undid several shirt buttons revealing a cadaverous torso, lit a cigarette, stretched himself out on the settee and adjusted the cushion under his head so that he was more comfortable.

It was while the official was lying on the settee, waiting for his black-eyed houri to join him – his mind still sustaining the romantic delusion – that Mr Effendi returned home after being delayed on a country road by a minor mechanical fault in his car. Mrs Effendi had locked herself in the kitchen, wondering whether she should remain in her house or seek refuge in that of her neighbour.

Mr Effendi was surprised to see the lights burning in his house, but thinking that his wife had fallen asleep, opened the door using his own key. He was shocked to see a man sprawled on the settee. After a moment of bewilderment he realized who the man was. So the man had trapped him! But what business did he have to lie on the settee in his house, obscenely displaying the front of his torso? Did his wife permit him? Another man in his house while he was away! In a paroxysm of rage he rushed out of the house to call his assistant Charles – an ex-boxer still in fine fettle – who was unloading the bags from the car in the street. He shouted to Charles that there was a 'dog' in the house who must be 'killed'.

Mr Hill quickly ran to the table and from a file in his bag took out the notice.

Mr Effendi and Charles stormed in.

'You are supposed to be in India!' Mr Hill shouted, waving the notice and retreating to the bedroom door.

'India!' Mr Effendi said, coming to a sudden standstill.

'Yes. Look at this notice. You can stay longer here.'

'India … ? Stay longer here?'

Mr Hill went up to Mr Effendi and showed him the notice. He pointed to the words at the bottom of the page: 'Gone to India for a visit'.

'It true,' Mrs Effendi said, coming to stand beside her husband (after watching apprehensively from the kitchen door). 'No more hiding away. Mr Hill do us favour.'

'Oh! Oh!' Mr Effendi burst out laughing. 'So you have tricked your seniors at the office. Wonderful! Wonderful!'

Mr Hill laughed too, but at his own cleverness in foiling an irate husband.

'Come, sit down, Mr Hill. Let's have coffee,' Mr Effendi said.

'Thank you,' Mr Hill said, placing the notice safely into the bag and looking at Mrs Effendi going towards the kitchen.

In the Train

'Hurry Hazel!' he shouted as she raced across the platform towards the carriage door which he held open. He grabbed her outstretched hand as she reached him, pulled her into the carriage as the train began to move. He held her hand firmly and looked at her slender pink-clad perfumed body: her heart was pounding and her breath coming in warm gusts, her whole form a wind-blown anemone.

He had first seen her at the station in Lenasia. She was standing on the platform, a solitary figure looking across the railway lines towards the buildings of the sprawling military camp partly hidden by the foliage of giant blue-gum trees. The morning was fresh and the dew dazzled on the neatly trimmed trees on the platform and the beds of pansies and carnations. His eyes were set ablaze by the bright yellow of her dress and the blue chiffon scarf over her head and knotted under her chin. For a moment he stood still as though some strange communion was established between him and her, a communion at once subtle and clear, and then he lost sight of her as the shrill whistle sounded and commuters rushing towards the opened doors surrounded him.

The next morning he found himself seated opposite her in the carriage. While she turned the pages of a magazine he took the opportunity of looking at her. She was dainty, about fifteen or sixteen years old. Her hair, partly covered by a scarf, was honey-brown in colour; her complexion a tawny sand. And when she raised her eyes as the train stopped to gather more passengers, he saw that they were a greenish grey.

When the train reached Johannesburg he opened the door for her and her 'Thank you' and smile dispelled any diffidence in him. He followed her and asked her where she worked.

'Why, do you want to employ me?' she asked laughingly. And he laughed as accord was established between them.

Every morning Farid went to the station earlier than usual and waited for Hazel's arrival. How his heart frolicked to see her or, when she was late, how it panicked that the train would come and he would have to board it without her. In the train he sat beside her, or opposite her, assured of her presence, involved in her being, and the other passengers seemed vague, undefined dream-forms.

Their love flowered in the train as it sped to Johannesburg. Farid found happiness in little things: in the sight of Hazel's lacquered nails, her squashed handkerchief in her hand, in the brooch that clung to her. And Hazel loved Farid's gaiety, his wit, the gush of words that escaped from his lips.

Farid worked in the office of a property owner. He collected the rent from the tenants and kept records. He left the office at two in the afternoon. Hazel worked in the office of a retailer in Market Street. She lived with her aunt in Lenasia. Her parents were in Cape Town.

Usually the two lovers travelled home in the late afternoon train with the other commuters (Farid having stopped over at friends until it was time to meet Hazel). But there were days when Hazel was not busy in the office and her employer permitted her to leave early. On such days they took the three o'clock train home. The first class compartment in the carriage with its four seats would be empty. The train took forty minutes to reach their destination, and those forty minutes of confinement in a moving carriage were blissful. The carriage became their alcove of love, a mobile alcove untouched by the constantly receding world beyond the windows.

One day when the train reached Mayfair station the carriage door was thrust open and two men in military uniforms entered and sat down on the two vacant seats. The two lovers were puzzled as the carriage was not for whites. The train began to move. Farid and Hazel looked at each other, annoyed that there were others to intrude on their privacy.

Both men were tall, their faces reddened by exposure to the sun. Their hair, blond and thread-like, was cut very short and one of them had a brush-like moustache. They did not look at Farid or Hazel; they looked at each other, grinning and smirking.

The train gathered momentum. One of the men kicked the other's boot, and the second, suddenly, flung himself onto his partner and held him in a firm embrace. They grimaced and began to bite each other playfully, on the neck, the ears, cheeks. They pushed and jostled, trying to unseat each other. They hugged each other like two large bears – clawing, gripping, twisting and growling. When they were tired from their wrestling they stopped until they had regained their breath. And then they flung themselves on each other again. They fell on the floor and rolled in the limited space, all the time biting and growling like two playful animals. On the floor their wrestling took a different turn – they tried to grab at each other's genitals. They grimaced like puppets. Then one of them seemed to get the better of his fellow and fixed himself to the rear of his partner and performed the motion of coition like a dog.

Farid and Hazel sat mutely, enmeshed.

The two men did not stop in their play until the train began to slow down. By then they were out of breath; their military uniforms no longer spruce, their faces red; but their grimaces remained. As soon as the train came to a halt in Lenasia they jumped out, raced across the platform, jumped down, leaped over the rails and ran towards the military camp.

Farid and Hazel alighted. They walked over the platform without saying a word or holding hands. When they had crossed the overhead bridge and were a short distance away from the station, they began to run.

Mr Moonreddy

EVERYONE IN LENASIA, A TOWNSHIP on the perimeter of Johannesburg, considered Mr Moonreddy to be a gentleman. He was a small mild-tempered man with glossy black hair. He was very proud of his hair, and every morning when he got up and dressed with meticulous care, it was his hair that received fastidious devotion. There was an invariable ritual he followed in its grooming. He would fill the wash-basin with warm water, pour in a spoonful of Dettol or other antiseptic, pour into the hollow of his left palm a pink shampoo and briskly work up a thick lather on his head. He would then wash off the soapy froth and dry his hair with a clean towel and an electric hair-dryer. After that he would rub into his scalp expensive hair oils (Mr Moonreddy was very careful in the selection of hair preparations: 'Only the best,' he would say with a golden-toothed smile); he would then comb his long hair backwards and with deft fingers set the waves. Finally, he would shower his head with a sweet-scented spray to keep his hair firmly in place for the day. And, before setting out on the long walk to the station to take the train to Johannesburg where he worked at an hotel as a waiter, he would glance at himself in the mirror, and smile approvingly.

Mr Moonreddy was a bachelor and lived with the widow Moodley and her ten-year-old daughter in the area mock-humorously called 'Dry Bones' in Lenasia on account of the rough-and-ready, monotonously homogeneous, rectangular houses and the dusty rutted roads. The widow Moodley was a spry little woman of about forty, pleasant, gossipy, very clean, with a strong penchant for maroon-coloured saris. Her hair was always neatly gathered in a bun at the back of her head, with a comb or two to keep it in place. Mr Moonreddy's first requirement as far as housekeeping went was cleanliness, and he often boasted that the widow Moodley was one of the few women who kept the customs of the 'dirty Tamils' out of her home. The widow's daughter was a weak-eyed girl, but very industrious, and Mr Moonreddy would occasionally bring her a delicacy, such as a grilled lobster, from the hotel where he worked.

That Mr Moonreddy was a waiter was no fault of his. He was convinced that he had been cut out for a better vocation in life, but that he had been the victim of 'unpropitious circumstances, unpropitious circumstances, gentlemen.' He uttered these words in the local bar one day in the company of some teachers who frequented the place. The 'unpropitious circumstances' happened to be the poverty of his parents. They had slaved in the sugar-cane fields of Natal, and they had found it hard, with their low resources, to keep their only son in school. As a consequence he had left after Standard Four ('Year after year I topped class, and my teacher said it was real tragedy that I leave') and his education had come to an end. Later, after a few years, an 'inauspicious period' set in with the death of his parents; he was left to fend for himself. He became a 'waiter by profession' and moved from Natal to Johannesburg.

'Gentlemen,' he said to the group of teachers over whisky and soda, 'you see me, Mr Moonreddy, a self-made man, not educated like you, not belonging to intellectual class, but a waiter. Yet a waiter of distinction.'

'A waiter of distinction,' someone said in a voice tinged with an ironic undertone. 'Let us drink to him.'

They swilled their whisky with evident satisfaction. One of the teachers offered to buy another round of drinks. Mr Moonreddy stood up and said: 'No, gentlemen, you not buy me drink. Let it never be said that I cannot buy teacher colleagues drink.' He placed his hand in his trouser pocket and produced a wad of notes. The teachers looked at the money enviously, for they were a poorly paid lot.

'I am fully aware of the financial circumstances of gentlemen teachers. Allow me the pleasure.' And he flourished the notes and called the steward.

'Steward, come here, hurry up!'

The steward, a lazy, thin fellow, shuffled up, and Mr Moonreddy ordered whisky and soda for all.

One of the teachers, seeking a bit of amusement, inquired slyly: 'Mr Moonreddy, when the whites at the hotel call you, do they show any kind of respect?'

Mr Moonreddy was outraged. He eyed the man for a moment with glazed tipsy eyes.

'Look here, man. I am not any Tom or Dick. I am Mr Moonreddy of Lawrence Hotel, you understand?'

'And I am Mr Ram of Republic Bar,' said the steward, coming up with the drinks.

'Mr Moonreddy, don't talk to him. You are a born gentleman,' someone said in an attempt to pacify him.

But Mr Moonreddy was not easily soothed. He could not weather deprecatory remarks; they harrowed some rawness inside him. He swallowed the liquor at one swig and stared at the empty glass as though it had offended him.

The teachers moved off to play a game of billiards. Mr Moonreddy sat meditatively for a while in his chair, then rose, went to the barman, bought a double whisky, drank it while standing, and went out.

Outside the bar there was the odour of rain in the air. The lights in the few shops shone weakly. Mr Moonreddy went homewards, swaying and lurching along. When he reached Mrs Moodley's door, it began to rain.

Mr Moonreddy's hours of duty at the Lawrence Hotel stretched from about eleven in the morning to ten at night, and he usually took the last train at night to Lenasia. In the train a number of other waiters rode with him. He rarely condescended to speak to them in a friendly way, and whatever conversation existed was of a cool distant kind: he would offer them cigarettes or borrow matches, briefly comment on the weather or make a curt remark about the drunk white guard. As the train journey was short, Mr Moonreddy's reserve never really caused any offence. As soon as they reached Lenasia station, they went their several ways.

One night as Mr Moonreddy reached the widow Moodley's door he heard the fierce howling of dogs down the road, and then the prolonged, high-pitched, agonized wail of a dog, its body torn by the pack. Mr Moonreddy stood outside for a moment, his figure enveloped in shadow. An infinite sense of pain and bitterness gushed over him; the cry of the dog seemed to find some accord in his soul; it triggered off reverberations of pain. And when he entered the house and crept into bed, he felt a sort of unhappiness he had never experienced before.

Three nights later he again heard the cry of a dog and he again experienced the anguish, as though his very body was being attacked by the vicious brutes. He stood in the road, undergoing this violent experience, rent by canine teeth. And when the dog's cries ceased, Mr Moonreddy was surprised to find himself in a quiet road, with the houses looming around him, and the coolness of tears on his cheeks.

And when, on subsequent nights, he again heard the cry of a dog his feelings underwent a subtle change. There was still the feeling of fellowship with the animal, of sympathy, but an element of pleasure crept into it, of schadenfreude, a peculiar insidious kind of pleasure. It seemed as if he experienced a state of catharsis, a purging of pressures within. If he happened to be in bed and heard the cry, he would jump out and fling the window wide open, so as to capture within him every note of anguish, and listen as though he were entranced by the score of some terrible symphony.

A month later, as the widow Moodley was busy with her household chores, there was a knock on the door. When she opened the door she found a young man who informed her that he had been instructed to deliver a dog for Mr Moonreddy. She was puzzled. 'I can't see what he wants to do with a dog,' she said. The dog was tied to a pole in the yard.

Mr Moonreddy cared for his dog as he had cared for no one else in his life. He fed it with the choicest of meat; from the hotel he would bring fried chicken. Mrs Moodley and her daughter were not highly amused by Mr Moonreddy's fad of feeding his dog food that was suitable for human consumption, and she was tempted to appropriate some of the money he had given her to buy various 'pets' delights'.

Early in the morning Mr Moonreddy would give his dog exercise, take it into the veld for a run. He would encourage the dog to run after rabbits and wild meercats. Although the dog never managed to catch them, Mr Moonreddy would watch the dog enthusiastically through a pair of binoculars. He spent a great deal of time and effort teaching the dog certain commands, and especially instilling hatred for other dogs. On the way home after the morning's expedition, Mr Moonreddy would encourage his dog to attack other dogs along the road, but he would not relax the leash; he felt satisfied with the dog's fierce tugging and the eager willingness to obey him.

One night, after he had returned home, he took his dog and furtively went out. It was a dark night. There was a refreshing breeze. He passed through the roads of 'Dry Bones', skirted the shopping centre and entered the area where the wealthier class of Indians live. He stood under a tree on the pavement and with eager eyes scanned the street. Then he saw a shadow moving towards him at a trot, and his heart beat with wild elation. His nervous fingers glided over the neck of his dog as the words stumbled out of his mouth: 'Go! Go! Kill!' He removed the leash and the dog bounded away towards the running shadow; when the shadow came under a street lamp Mr Moonreddy saw that it was a little dog. Instantly his great Alsatian was upon it. The little dog let out a howl, and then a multitude of sharp cries as the fangs gored into the flesh. Mr Moonreddy stood under a tree, clutching a branch, bathed in sweat, tears running down his cheeks, overwhelmed by a complex feeling of pleasure and pain.

While Mr Moonreddy stood under the tree, he was unaware of a man who came out of his house and threw several stones at his dog. It was only when there was complete silence for some time and his dog was brushing against him, that he regained a complete sense of his own identity. When he had sufficiently recovered, he went home.

Early next morning he went into the yard and was stunned – the dog was dead. There was a scarlet band of congealed blood near the dog's ear. An involuntary scream escaped from his lips, a scream that brought the widow and her daughter running from the house.

Mr Moonreddy choked; his eyes welled with tears; words stuck in his throat as he pointed helplessly at the dog and at the two females. The widow and her daughter froze at the accusing finger. They fled into the house. Later they heard Mr Moonreddy entering his room, closing the door and locking it.